LITTLE BOY LOST

LITTLE BOY LOST
Lesley Egan

Published for the Crime Club
by
Doubleday & Company, Inc.
Garden City, New York
1983

All of the characters in this book are fictitious,
and any resemblance to actual persons,
living or dead, is purely coincidental.

Library of Congress Cataloging in Publication Data

Egan, Lesley, 1921–
Little Boy Lost.

I. Title.
PS3562.I515L5   1983   813'.54
ISBN 0-385-18840-4
Library of Congress Catalog Card Number: 82-25166

First Edition

This one is for
Virginia
for old times' sake.

And after all what is a lie? 'Tis but
The truth in masquerade.
                                    —DON JUAN
                                    Lord Byron

LITTLE BOY LOST

Jesse drifted into Central Courtroom Three at a few minutes before ten. There were a couple of bailiffs chattering desultorily at one of the rear doors; otherwise the courtroom was empty except for Bill Carlow, of Carlow and Weekes, sitting at one of the tables before the bench. Jesse went over to sit down beside him, and Carlow nodded at him grumpily.

"And I suppose," he said, "it's the same with you. Cut-and-dried divorce, fifteen minutes to get it on file with the court—and I've got an appointment at eleven-thirty. It would have to be Dalrymple. Any bets on when we'll get out of here?"

"That's right," said Jesse amiably. Dalrymple was notoriously late in convening court; gossips said that he had to cure a hangover every morning, but as he was a bachelor nobody really knew. Like Carlow, Jesse had a cut-and-dried divorce suit to present the court, but he hadn't anything else on his agenda except the proofreading of a will when he got back to the office, until an appointment with a new client at two-thirty.

A minute later Carlow said with feeling, "Hell and damnation! Wouldn't you know!"

Jesse looked up from rummaging in his briefcase. One of the bailiffs was shepherding a man through the rear door of the court, and another man accompanied them, a big man with rough-hewn features, in a rumpled business suit. "For God's sake," said Carlow, "an arraignment. That's Carney from Central Homicide. They'll take that first—we won't get out of here until noon, damn it."

"And that's Honeycutt," said Jesse. "Suppose the bench'll appoint a public defender."

Carlow grunted. Jesse regarded Carl Honeycutt with faint interest. He was a heavy-shouldered, nondescript man in his fifties, neatly dressed in a gray suit and white shirt; he looked morose. "Funny case," said Carlow. "I suppose. Handful of nothing, legally speaking. But a funny one."

It had been a slightly off-beat case, spread in the papers ten days ago. Carl Honeycutt had lived a humdrum everyday existence with a nondescript wife for over twenty years; he had a barbershop in downtown L.A., and he'd never had so much as a moving violation ticket. Six months after his wife died of cancer last year, he had remarried; and a couple of weeks ago he had gone berserk with a shotgun and killed his new wife, her brother and sister-in-law, and a neighbor who had attempted to reason with him.

"Never even known to tie one on," said Carlow. "A funny one all right. Makes you wonder about people."

Jesse said sleepily, "Catalysts. Like in chemistry."

"What?"

"A meets B, they have a nice cozy smooth relationship—marriage, friendship, business, whatever. A meets C, or B meets D, bang, there's an explosion. Like catalytic agents in chemistry."

"Oh," said Carlow. "As good an explanation as any. But damn it, the damn judge is ten minutes late already—I won't get out of here until noon—"

"Annoying," agreed Jesse. Three minutes later the judge finally appeared, and of course took the arraignment first; the homicide officer gave brief testimony, and it took some twenty minutes and delayed the other business of the court. Carlow got his divorce suit on the agenda in another fifteen minutes and departed fuming; Jesse didn't get out of court until a quarter of twelve. Over lunch at a coffee shop on Western Avenue, he ruminated vaguely about Honeycutt: a queer enough case and thank God

it was no business of his; but people did come all sorts and
shapes, and were set in motion by, perhaps, the catalytic agents
as well as other things.

He got back to the office on Wilshire at one-twenty, and the
will was on his desk for proofreading; his twin secretaries, the
good-looking blondes, Jean and Jamesina Gordon, were eminently efficient.

*   *   *

The new client was punctual at two-thirty; Jean ushered her in.
She had made the appointment three days ago: a Mrs. Charlene
Garland.

Jesse rose to greet her and settled her in the client's chair beside his desk. She was a good-looking woman, not young, perhaps in her forties, but well and neatly dressed in a navy suit.
She had dark hair sprinkled with a little gray, and a figure just
slightly plump. She was carrying a book as well as her outsized
navy handbag.

"And what can I do for you, Mrs. Garland?" he asked
pleasantly.

She studied him for a moment before speaking. She would
have been a very pretty girl twenty years ago; she had a
roundish face with a generous mouth, wide-set blue eyes. She
said unexpectedly, "If old Mr. Halliday had still been alive, I
wouldn't be here—he'd have done something whether I went to
him or not. But he died last year. And I don't know but what I
want a private detective instead of a lawyer—but Mrs. Christiansen said I ought to see a lawyer—and I really don't know
what a lawyer could do, but maybe you will."

"Well, suppose you tell me what it's about and we'll see." Jesse
offered her a cigarette.

She took it, bent to his lighter, and sat back with a little sigh.
"You see, Mr. Falkenstein, you do have to think about money,
don't you? Without being mercenary or thinking about it all the
time—it is important, isn't it?"

"You have to think about it."

"Well—I'd better tell you something about my situation. So
you'll have the whole picture. I'm a widow—Bob was killed on

the job two years ago. He was in construction work. It was the company's fault—I needn't go into that—they were very fair, there wasn't any legal hassle, it was faulty equipment, and they made a good settlement, paid off the house and gave me a lump sum. Not that anything would be enough for losing Bob." The hand holding her cigarette was shaking slightly. "I'd gone back to work the year before—I'm a bookkeeper at Kelly and Howard, they're a big building materials outfit in the Valley—wholesale to construction firms mostly. We're getting along just fine, you see, with the settlement and the house paid for—but you have to think about money. I've got two children, Cindy's eighteen, and she'll graduate from high school in June, and Paul's sixteen. They'll both want to go to college, and"—she sighed sharply—"I didn't know any lawyers," she said, "except Mr. Halliday. And I went and saw Mr. Holden, and they just don't care—he as good as said he wouldn't and couldn't do anything, and I got mad—and a friend of mine said you'd been very good at getting a divorce for a friend of hers, so I thought—"

"Yes," said Jesse. Such were the random ways clients came to lawyers. He was letting her take her time.

"I don't know whether you know them—it was Halliday, Holden and Wirtz, but since Mr. Halliday died it's just the other two." Jesse had a nodding acquaintance with the firm, an old and prestigious one in Los Angeles.

"Mr. Halliday was an old friend of Uncle Tom's. He'd have done something—I don't know what. But at least he'd have been able to get Aunt Ruth to listen to him. I think. If anybody could." She uttered a short laugh and stabbed out her cigarette in the ashtray on the desk. "But as it is—Mr. Falkenstein, does the name Traxler mean anything to you? Do you remember anything about the Traxler kidnapping?"

Jesse spread his hands. "Should I? I'm afraid not—it doesn't ring any bells."

"Well, it's twenty-one years ago, of course. And it didn't make all the national headlines. I'll have to tell you all the background —I'm sorry to take up so much of your time—"

"No hurry, take your time and tell me whatever you think I should know."

"Yes. Well, Thomas Traxler—Uncle Tom—was my mother's older brother. He made a lot of money. It was—sort of, you could say, inadvertent. He and his partner, George Coleman, had a little tool-and-die business out in the Valley—Glendale—this was way back in the Depression. When the war started they converted to making small aircraft parts, and the business really took off—by the end of the war it was booming. And Coleman was a bachelor without any relatives, and he was killed in an accident and left his share of the business to Uncle Tom. There was—there is quite a lot of money, not just the business. Uncle Tom invested in land and real estate as well as stocks and so on, you see. Of course, the business was sold later but—there's still a lot of money. I'm getting ahead of myself, I'm sorry." She took a breath. "Uncle Tom and Aunt Ruth were married sometime just before the war began, around there, and neither of them was exactly young then. And they were married for nearly fifteen years before Tommy was born—their little boy. I expect you can guess how they idolized him. Looking back, I can see how they spoiled him—how maybe he'd have grown up to be an obnoxious spoiled darling—you know? He had everything. They had an English nanny for him and all the toys—the clothes—I don't really remember much about him," said Charlene Garland, "except that he was rather a shy little boy—and so very polite, in an old-fashioned way—the way he'd been taught. You see, Aunt Ruth is—was—English. Her mother was widowed quite young, and they came here when she married an American—it must be fifty years ago, but Aunt Ruth's so proud of being English, she's —kept it up. Afternoon tea and the accent and everything— everything you can imagine, English. She taught Tommy little pieces he had to recite for guests—people haven't done that since the nineties, have they?—but she did—and that's not irrelevant. I'm getting to the point, Mr. Falkenstein," and she gave him a faint smile. "Little nursery rhymes. They—Uncle Tom and Aunt Ruth—gave us the reception when Bob and I were married, that was—just before it happened, twenty-one years ago. They'd bought the house about five years before, it was when the Mt. Olympus Estates were being opened, you know that exclusive area—" One of the most exclusive and expensive residential areas, that was indeed, in upper Hollywood, adjoining the equally exclusive Trousdale Estates in Beverly Hills. "It was a lovely reception, they paid for everything, they'd always been so good to Mother and me—and to get back to the money, you see, I know very well that Uncle Tom would have left Mother something in his will—and possibly me too, he liked Bob. You see, Mother had been divorced from my father since I was ten. But the month after Bob and I were married, there was—the kidnapping. Tommy was kidnapped. Uncle Tom paid the ransom, but they never got him back. They never knew what happened to him. It was terrible—a terrible thing to happen. He was five and a half."

"I suppose the FBI was on it?" said Jesse.

"Yes, and the local police. They never found out a thing. I don't really know much about that part of it—Bob was working for a firm in Fresno then, we lived there for five years before we came back to the L.A. area, both the children were born there. But it was just terrible for them—you can imagine. Uncle Tom paid the ransom, a hundred thousand dollars, but they never got Tommy back. I think the FBI was sure he'd been killed—well, kidnappers usually do murder children, don't they?"

"Not always."

"But usually. And he was five and a half, he could have told something about the people who took him. But—it all came to nothing. It was awful. About six months later, I think it was, there was a body found—a child's body—but it couldn't be definitely identified. There'd been another child reported missing about the same time Tommy was kidnapped, and the police thought the body could have been his as well as Tommy's. It was just left up in the air, you see?"

"Yes."

"Well—" She took a long breath. "I'm sorry to be so longwinded, but you've got to have the background. It just about killed Uncle Tom. He'd been in his fifties when Tommy was born, and it was as if he had lost everything that meant anything to him. He just seemed to lose interest in life altogether, he didn't care what happened. And to come to the money, Mr. Falkenstein, I know he'd probably have left Mother something in the will, but you see, they had a row. A fight. They were both quick-tempered people, and they—sort of flared up at each other. And he—" She grimaced. "It was silly."

"About what?"

"Well, the psychics. It was silly," said Charlene Garland. "You see, Aunt Ruth never gave up hope about Tommy. She wouldn't believe he was dead—that that body could have been his. And she kept going to all the fortune tellers—calling themselves psychics, sensitives, you know—I suppose one in a hundred of them is honest, but mostly they're just telling people what they want to hear for the money, aren't they? And some of them told her Tommy was dead, but some of them told her he was alive and eventually she'd have him back—and Mother told Uncle Tom he ought to put his foot down and stop her going to them, it wasn't only a waste of money but it was so bad for her, and he said anything that gave her comfort was all right with him, and they had a row—and I know that eventually they'd have made it up, but in the meantime he changed his will and left everything to Aunt Ruth, and then a few months later he died of a heart attack. He was only sixty-three—but he'd—just lost any interest in life."

"I see," said Jesse. "And is she still going to see the psychics?"

"Oh"—she made an impatient gesture—"no, not for years, I don't think. She didn't exactly turn into a recluse—she used to entertain a lot, and she stopped doing that, but she's still got her bridge club and shopping, and sometimes she goes to the theater —oddly enough she was never annoyed with Mother, and she always treated us like family, you know? She's always given the children and me nice birthday and Christmas presents, and she'd invite Bob and me for dinner sometimes. Like that. And after all, we were the only family she has and—" she hesitated.

"And you were pretty sure she'd have left you a bundle of the money?" he filled in for her. "Do you know how your uncle left it?"

"Yes. It's all in trust, with his lawyers—Halliday, Holden and Wirtz, only now Mr. Halliday's dead. He was an old friend of Uncle Tom's. They handle all the money, but it's not tied up any way, she can leave it however she wants. I remember her saying that after Uncle Tom died, when the will was read, and she even said then that of course it should come to us, she hadn't any relatives left at all and it was Uncle Tom's money and we were his relatives."

"Fair enough," said Jesse. He slid down a little further in his desk chair, long legs stretched out. "So what's the snag?"

She looked very angry suddenly. "That's what I'm coming to. She—I don't know how to tell you, it's so absurd—and so wild. She thinks she's got Tommy back."

"And how did that happen, for God's sake?"

Charlene Garland took the cigarette he offered her. "Oh, it's wild," she said. "And he's got to be—he is—the most flagrant imposter—but he's clever, oh, he's clever. He's got Aunt Ruth absolutely convinced, and she's furious at me because I don't believe it. There." All this time she'd been nursing the book on her lap, and now she laid it on his desk and sat back. "It started with that. So he says."

Jesse looked at the book. It still wore its dust jacket in pristine condition; it was a fairly new-looking, hard-cover book entitled *Unsolved Mysteries of the Twentieth Century,* by James Gilchrist, and bore the name of a well-known publisher.

She looked at it bitterly, and then suddenly she laughed rather harshly. "After all," she said, "I don't want you to think she's an absolute fool, Mr. Falkenstein. She's got some reason to believe him—only she won't see—well!" She drew strongly on the cigarette. "That"—and she nodded at the book—"has an account of the kidnapping. I remember her telling me how she gave an interview to the author—that was a couple of years ago. It's just a —a—rehash of the facts, the police work and so on. But there's a photograph of Tommy, and of the house. And when she had this letter—to put it briefly, he claims that he picked up the book just casually, and the photograph of the house triggered his memory. He says he'd always had these vague memories of a place and people where he'd lived as a little boy, but it wasn't until he saw that picture that they all came together for him and he remembered a lot more. He's told her—" She was silent and put a hand to her head. "In a way you can't blame her, Mr. Falkenstein. Of course she wanted desperately to believe him, but what he's told her—I saw that letter, and it was clever—he's so clever. He could tell her things—I can't imagine how, where he got the facts—things not in that book, little personal things. The things a child would remember. He told her the names he had for his favorite toys, there was a big stuffed bear, and a rocking horse—and he told her about the dog they had, a golden cocker named Bonnie, and how he used to play with her. He told her some of the little pieces she'd taught him to recite for company—he claimed to remember that, when she served tea out of the silver service, and saying verses for company—and he told her what he called the nanny. A pet name—he always called her Judy because she told him stories about Punch and Judy—and he told her the nursery had yellow curtains with an animal print on them—and there was a furry rug in front of the fireplace there. And how the nanny read him poetry about the bells of London—and told him stories about when she was a little girl in Barnstaple in England."

"Very interesting," said Jesse. "And I take it that was all true?"

"You just can't imagine how she reacted to that letter. She'd never accepted that Tommy was dead—and here was a letter from him, she had to believe it was from him—oh, it was so cleverly done—"

"Tell me what you remember about the letter. You saw it?"

She nodded. "She was so excited—she phoned me at work, I had to come and see it for myself, she just knew this was Tommy! It was—all very slickly done. It was phrased—oh, humble, if you gather what I mean, he wasn't claiming anything at all, he was just so interested himself in these memories the story had aroused in him, and they were so vivid he couldn't help thinking they must mean something, but he wasn't suggesting he really could be her long lost son, he just thought perhaps she would be interested too—and coming out with all of this, how he remembered sitting on a man's lap and playing with a big gold watch—Uncle Tom's half hunter, it was an heirloom from his grandfather, of course—and reciting 'Hickety pickety, my black hen, She lays eggs for gentlemen'—and Bonnie—and Judy —how it all seemed to come back to him all at once when he saw the picture of the house—oh Lord, you can see she had some reason! She was so excited—"

"And where did the plausible gent say he'd been since the age of five and a half?" asked Jesse. "Suggest the kidnappers found him such a charming child they kept him?"

She laughed shakily. "Well, even that's plausible—what he says, I mean. He just doesn't know, he can't give any explanation. He was brought up in a religious orphanage in Long Beach, and he says they never found out where he came from— he'd been abandoned apparently, by whoever had been looking after him, and he doesn't remember much about that at all, just a vague Uncle Bernie and Aunt Mae who went away. He didn't even—in the letter, ask to see her, and that was the cleverest thing of all, because, of course, she couldn't wait to see him—"

"Letter sent locally?"

"Yes—Hollywood. It was a motel out on Sunset. Of course she couldn't wait to meet him. I told her she should be careful, it sounded like a trick to me, and she said who but her own Tommy would remember all that? She called him right away and asked him to the house—and, Mr. Falkenstein, I wasn't there but she told me about it afterward—she was so triumphant that I'd been wrong and she'd been right!—when he got to the house, he asked her right away if there hadn't been a different picture over the mantel in the living room, the one he remembered had a wagon and horses and cows—and of course she had to take him all over the house, and especially to show him the nursery—she's kept it all exactly as it was, you know, all Tommy's toys and his bed and clothes—"

"Morbid," said Jesse.

"I'll agree with you every time," she said tiredly. "But there it is and he recognized the toys, he said he'd called the stuffed bear Huggy and the rocking horse was Dapple Peter—and he said that door went into Judy's room past the bathroom—they'd enclosed the back bath and put a door on either side of it to make a sort of nursery suite when Tommy was born, and they got the English nanny. And he told her how the housekeeper used to make him a kind of cookie he especially liked, a crunchy orange cookie—they were orange meringues, Tommy was crazy about them—"

"Very interesting," said Jesse. "And very circumstantial. You think—you thought right away—he's a fake."

"Mr. Falkenstein," and she sat up straighter, looking at him steadily, "if I could somehow believe that Tommy wasn't killed, that for whatever unimaginable reason the kidnappers just abandoned him and he ended up in an orphanage—as Jerry Smith, he says, the only name the orphanage knew—and a boy five and a half years old would know his own name, after all—but if I could believe this really is Tommy, I'd be only too happy for Aunt Ruth. But it's just impossible. I said that body could never be identified, but I think the FBI was sure it was Tommy, and Uncle Tom accepted that he was dead. And at the time, if he'd been just abandoned, a child that age would be able to tell his name, about his home, he'd have been identified then. This claim that a picture in a book triggered all these memories—it's just impossible."

"Little farfetched," agreed Jesse. "You said she called you, had to show you the letter. Family feud patched up, I take it—you said—"

"Oh, Aunt Ruth was never angry at Mother, as I told you—that was Uncle Tom. And, just as I said—"

"She'd probably made a will leaving you and your mother most of the money."

"Mother died last year. If she had, she probably made a new will then. I couldn't say about that. But I could have a pretty good guess that she's made a new one now," said Charlene Garland. "And I don't apologize for sounding mercenary, Mr. Falkenstein—but aside from anything else it is pretty damned galling to see that smooth con artist smirking at her, living in that house, probably running up bills on her credit cards, and calling himself by her name—and knowing she's probably left him everything, while we get left out—and it was Uncle Tom's money—and—"

Jesse sat up. "She's moved him into the house? Handed over money to him?"

"Naturally! She's accepted him as her darling Tommy come back to her—she always knew he was still alive somewhere—and nothing's too good for Tommy, especially since they were apart all those years because those terrible people were so wicked—"

"My God," said Jesse. "And you say she's not a fool, Mrs. Garland? What explanation has she dreamed up for the kidnappers not returning him twenty-one years ago?"

"She hasn't. She just says people that wicked would do anything, and they were just jealous of people like them who were happy and had money. Or maybe they were frightened of getting caught and just left him in the street somewhere. And maybe they'd kept him drugged so he'd forgotten most of what he knew, even his name. And isn't it the most wonderful, miraculous thing that he happened to read dear Mr. Gilchrist's book and see the photograph, so he began to remember all those things."

"My dear God," said Jesse. "You said she was annoyed at you for telling her to be careful. Are you still on speaking terms?"

"Not since last week," said Charlene Garland. "That's why I'm here—though I did consider a private detective instead. She loves to show him off, you see—and oh, isn't he putting up the beautiful act with her! The humble, wide-eyed innocent, can't believe he's found his own mama after the lonely years in the orphanage—so deferential, so polite—she loves it. Uncle Tom must be whirling in his grave. She insisted he move into the house, she's bought him a car, I think she's undoubtedly giving him an allowance and God knows what else. And—"

"Any resemblance?" asked Jesse.

"To a five-year-old boy? There's a picture in there," and she nodded at the book. "You can judge for yourself. He's blond—so was Tommy, but lots of blond children turn brown-haired when they grow up. Tommy would be twenty-six and a half, and he might be about that or older—he's got one of those boyish faces. Somewhere he's learned to talk decent grammar, and he's got good manners. He might be anybody, Mr. Falkenstein. But he can't be Tommy Traxler. Poor Tommy's been dead for twenty-one years, almost for certain. Everybody but Aunt Ruth accepted that. And I went to see Mr. Holden, and I don't suppose he likes it either, but he just said frankly that there's nothing he or anyone can do about it. I don't think he's much interested. The trust comes to an end when she dies, and she's sixty-seven and she has a heart condition. I liked Mr. Halliday, and he'd have done something—he'd have been horrified, he'd have put that con artist through the third degree, showed Aunt Ruth how impossible it is—but he's gone, and there's nothing I can do at all. I certainly haven't covered up the way I feel, but there wasn't any point in having an open row. I've just been trying to persuade her to—well, make some investigation of this Jerry Smith's background, if any discrepancy showed up—"

"Yes, she's taking him on faith, isn't she? You finally had a row?"

"Oh, with a vengeance!" said Charlene Garland. "She asked us all to tea last Sunday—I told you she's very punctilious about keeping up English traditions. Cindy and Paul begged off, and I didn't blame them, but I thought as long as I could still talk to her I might reach her somehow, and I went. There was the famous silver tea service Mr. Smith claims to remember, and the usual cucumber sandwiches and weak tea and all—no, he wasn't there, she said, of course young people liked to make their own friends and she'd told him to feel free to bring them home, and that annoyed me enough—and then in the middle of tea Mrs. Christiansen came in, and that—" Suddenly she laughed. "It was funny in a way because she's the last person in the world you'd expect to start a fight. She's one of Aunt Ruth's oldest friends,

one of her bridge club members, and a very nice woman really
—one of those plump, amiable, woolly old ladies who calls everybody dear—you can't imagine them actually disliking anyone
or losing their tempers, so it was rather as if a pet lamb had suddenly turned and bit you—she came burbling in and Aunt Ruth
poured her some tea and went on talking about Tommy. And
Mrs. Christiansen feels the way I do about it, I knew that, but I
don't think she'd ever said anything to Aunt Ruth except vaguely.
So it was like a thunderbolt when she said Aunt Ruth should
take shame, mentioning that thieving imposter in front of Tom's
niece—and, well, it developed into quite a row indeed, and I'm
afraid I lost my temper. We're neither of us welcome there again,
and I drove Mrs. Christiansen home—she only lives a couple of
blocks away—and we blew off steam to each other, and she said
I ought to have a lawyer. To safeguard my interests is how she
put it." Charlene looked at him drearily. "Well, there it is, and
just what a lawyer could do about it I haven't an idea, but I feel
better having told you."

"Umm," said Jesse, lighting another cigarette, "and a very in-
triguing little tale it is, Mrs. Garland. The point you made—she
had some reason for swallowing it, if it is pretty specious. Mr.
Smith got all that information somewhere. Where? Any ideas
occur to you?"

She shook her head. "A good many people would know all
that—Aunt Ruth's always talked about Tommy, and the kidnapping, a lot. But her friends—"

"What about servants?"

"Yes, there's a housekeeper and a man who does odd jobs and
chauffeurs her—she doesn't drive. But all the servants she had at
the time were different. She doesn't keep a full-time maid now.
There's a cleaning service that sends people once a month, but
none of them—"

"Still, there'd be people who could have passed on that information?"

"Yes, certainly."

"The servants there at the time—" Jesse brooded over his
steepled hands. "Well, let me do some thinking on this, Mrs.

Garland. There may be—umm—steps we can take. I'll get back
to you and let you know what I come up with."

She stood up. "I've taken a lot of your time, and probably for
nothing. But if you can think of something—"

"Usually a way to beat the devil around a gate," said Jesse.
"Think I'll write her a nice formal letter asking for an interview
as your legal representative."

She laughed. "Good luck on that one!"

* * *

But it was an obvious first step to take, and he'd like to size
up the situation and the people for himself. He ushered her out
and stood in the outer office surveying his two secretaries, the
twin blondes, Jean and Jamesina Gordon. Evidently Ruth
Traxler was still in the Mt. Olympus house; he beckoned Jean
into his office and dictated a brief letter requesting an interview.

And it was getting on to five o'clock, with no more appoint-
ments scheduled. He picked up *Unsolved Mysteries of the
Twentieth Century*, reached for his hat and coat, and wished his
Gordons good night.

It had gone on being a wet and cold winter; it was drizzling
again today, and he switched on the heater in the Mercedes,
turning up Fairfax Avenue from Wilshire. They were well settled into the big house up Coldwater Canyon, on Paradise Lane,
now; it was farther to drive, but the relative isolation and space
were worth it. And Southern California needed the rain, but
Jesse was getting rather tired of it, and this was only Feb-
ruary; another couple of months to the end of the rainy season.

As he turned off Coldwater Canyon Drive to the short, dead-
end street, he saw their gateway lights beaming out at him in
the dusk, welcoming. The gates were open, which meant that
Athelstane was in. He slid the Mercedes into the garage alongside Nell's identical sedan, and went in the back door to warmth
and light in the old-fashioned big kitchen.

"You're early," said Nell in surprise. "I didn't hear the car—"
She was just putting a big bowl of salad into the refrigerator.

He bent to kiss her, his lovely Nell with her brown hair in its usual neat, thick chignon on her neck, dropped the book on the kitchen table and went to shed his coat. "Reasonably good day?"

"Need you ask, with all this rain? The offspring's been driving me up the wall—I wish I had that much energy."

Davy came pounding up, yelling, "Daddy! Daddy! Read about Mama Hubbard—read about kittens!" He thrust the book of nursery rhymes at Jesse's knees savagely, and Jesse swung them both up in his arms.

"Give me a minute to get my breath and sit down, big boy. All right."

"Everything's in the oven," said Nell. "We can have a nice leisurely cocktail hour."

"As if you ever drank cocktails."

"Well, I'm trying Dubonnet instead of sherry. It's got an interesting sort of taste."

In the living room there was a comforting, crackling fire going. Athelstane, the huge brindle mastiff, was stretched out on the hearth rug with his stomach exposed to the warmth, and Murteza, the seal-point Siamese (whose name meant the Lion of God in Arabic) was cozily ensconced on the mantel with front paws well tucked in under his chest. Davy clambered into Jesse's big armchair and opened the book importantly. "Mama Hubbard—no bones for the poor doggy—the funny doggy wears a coat—" At least he had graduated to some other traditional rhymes than the three little kittens, which had monopolized his conversation up to Christmas and the appearance of a new, large, expensive *Book of Nursery Favorites*. Discovering he was out of cigarettes, Jesse went back to the kitchen for a fresh pack and found Nell dipping into *Unsolved Mysteries of the Twentieth Century*.

"Hey," he said, "you can't have that until I've looked at it. It's something to do with a new client."

And settled down with Davy in the armchair he remembered that old rhyme and looked it up—"Hickety pickety, my black hen,/She lays eggs for gentlemen;/Gentlemen come every day/ To see what my black hen doth lay."

Davy looked up at him from the dewy innocence of twenty-two months. "Eggs," he announced wisely, "are in boxes at the store. Daddy, what's a hen?"

* * *

The book was a slick production. It was not James Gilchrist's maiden effort; listed before the title page were nine other books ranging from a volume of Victorian crimes, a popular history of gang warfare during prohibition, an anthology of Broadway musicals of the past forty years, through several pseudo autobiographies of theater personalities and one politician. At least these days ghost writers were not buried anonymously; they appeared on title pages as "by so and so with John Smith."

He leafed through *Unsolved Mysteries* desultorily: the Judge Crater case was covered, a couple of other mysterious vanishments including that of James Hoffa, several rather shapeless homicides only included, apparently, because the law had never brought charges. The writing was careful and good journalese, very professional.

And the Traxler case, when he found it, was sufficiently poignant and also shapeless. The two photographs illustrating the account told him little: black-and-white photographs, of an impressive two-story Spanish house above a terrace of lush lawn; the salon photograph of the head and shoulders of a small boy, fair and anonymous, just a small boy in an open-necked shirt.

A date in early September, twenty-one years ago. A family wealthy, but not fabulously so, just not socialites. Present in the house the housekeeper and her husband, man of all work and chauffeur, Albert and Thelma Dillon; the maid, Rose Shaw; the nursemaid, Katherine Drake. It had been a hot night, and the central air conditioning's motor had burned out the day before. The Traxlers, and the nursemaid, had had fans running in their bedrooms, and windows had been open all over the house. But the nurse maintained that she would have heard any noise from "Master Tommy's" room, separated from hers by a bathroom. No alarm had been raised until the next morning, when the child was found missing and a screen on a window in his room neatly cut out. Local police and the FBI had been called. A tap had been put on the phone; the servants had been examined, recent employees questioned: all the motions gone through. Some interest had been attached to a twelve-foot ladder recently used by a gardener to replace some roof tiles; it was the ladder used to reach the window of the nursery, which seemed to point to an inside job, but it had been left leaning against the side of the house, carelessly, for several days. No extraneous fingerprints had been found on the ladder or elsewhere; there were no leads in any direction. The servants had eventually been exonerated.

A ransom had been demanded, in a phone call recorded by the tap on the Traxler phone. It had been paid as asked, by the father, a hundred thousand dollars in unmarked bills, in a brief-case carried by Traxler to the pari-mutuel lines at Santa Anita racetrack, on a day when a handicap race was scheduled. The FBI had not been able to trace the man who snatched the brief-case from Traxler in the crowd.

There was a brief mention of the unidentified body found six months later, in Mission Canyon County Park. There was a brief account of an interview with Mrs. Ruth Traxler, who believed that her son was still alive somewhere—"a mother would know—" although she could give no rational explanation of her conviction.

There were no details of the kind the supposed Jerry Smith had given.

But Jesse thought he would like to talk to James Gilchrist.

Nell was upstairs reading in bed with Murteza snuggled down beside her, and Athelstane sound asleep on the floor on her side of the bed. Unprecedentedly, Jesse went to look in on Davy, who was also sound asleep, and thought soberly that although he had some money, and very nice too, it wasn't the kind of money that invited kidnapping.

2

At noon next day Jesse wandered into the LAPD, Hollywood, station house, and found Sergeant Andrew Clock talking with Detective Petrovsky over a report. "And what do you want?" asked Clock.

"Can't I offer to take my brother-in-law to lunch? How are Fran and the baby?"

"Flourishing," said Clock, suddenly sounding fatuous. "Both of 'em prettier every day."

"Good. I think we're supposed to have dinner with you some time this week. Can you tell me if there's anybody around here who was here twenty-one years ago?"

"That's a hell of a long time back. Why?"

Jesse explained, economically, and both Clock and Petrovsky were interested. "That's quite a con game—if it is," said Clock. "I suppose it's remotely possible, if unlikely—the woman must be a damned fool, but some women will be."

Petrovsky said, "We'd have been called on it first, our beat, but I suppose the Feds took over right away. I wonder if Garcia would remember anything about it, he's been here at least that long, I think."

Clock shrugged. "We can ask him. See if we can catch him now. The things you do get into, Jesse." He stood up from his desk chair, massaging his prominent jaw.

Sergeant Manuel Garcia was attached to Juvenile Division. Clock took Jesse down the hall to that office, and they found him just leaving to have lunch. Garcia was a paunchy big man in the late fifties, with a round, good-humored face and shrewd dark eyes. "We've got a new twist in a con game to pass on to you," said Clock, and introduced Jesse. "You recall anything about this snatch?"

Garcia listened to the story and said, "That one. Traxler. Yeah, I wasn't on it, but I recall this and that—we don't get a snatch every day of the week. The Feds took over, of course."

They took him to a coffee shop down on Fountain and he told Jesse what he remembered, which wasn't much. "I seem to recall Sergeant Rector was on it, don't remember who else—lessee, he retired a couple of years ago. There wasn't any handle on it at all, and from what emerged later—or didn't—the Feds never got anything either. It could have been an amateur job or a slick pro job, there just weren't any leads. You know the Feds, they shoved us out of it inside forty-eight hours, and all we knew after that was what was in the papers. The ransom got paid, but the kid never turned up."

"There was a body found a while later," said Jesse, "that could have been the Traxler boy. You remember that?"

Garcia shrugged over his sandwich. "Can't say I do."

"In Mission Canyon Park."

"Oh, I think that's somewhere out around Sherman Oaks—it'd be the Valley Division. Not our beat. I don't think the Feds ever got the smell of a lead on the snatch and we never heard anything more, and it dropped out of the newspapers, nobody ever got picked up or charged."

"Well, that's not much help," said Jesse.

"But that's a very sweet little con game, isn't it? It occurs to me, Falkenstein, that it's got to be a sort of inside job. Somebody who knew this woman would be apt to fall for it, somebody in a position to feed this Smith all that convincing information he handed her."

Jesse said, "Yes, and anybody's guess who. In twenty-one

years she'll have had a succession of servants, and evidently she talked about it to everybody—"

"But," said Clock, "it would have to be somebody fairly close to her, to know the names of those toys and so on."

"Possibly, but almost anybody who'd ever been in the house—"

"Somebody with a grudge on her?"

"Now don't reach so far, Andrew," said Jesse irritably. "You really don't have to look farther for motive than all the nice money, do you? Mr. Smith must be a smart actor, if the woman is a fool, to get her eating out of his hand like this—and I do wonder about Holden and Wirtz. Very reputable firm, I'd have thought—and there's also Mr. Gilchrist, of course. Well, thanks for nothing. I wonder if I'd get anything out of the Feds after all these years."

Clock, catching his thought, said, "There is that. Just because they never picked up anybody doesn't say they didn't have a few guesses. There was just no evidence to act on. If you could turn up anything to show that that body probably was the Traxler kid, or that they had any inside info pointing to homicide—"

Jesse said, "And I wonder if she'd listen to it—if so. Well, I can have a look around."

* * *

He had left Jean trying to reach the publisher on the phone. When he came into the office she said, "I finally got hold of an editor there. This Gilchrist lives in New Jersey, I got the address, but she says he's out here right now, doing some research —she didn't say on what. She thinks he'll be at a Holiday Inn somewhere in the L.A. area. I haven't found him yet."

"Surprise, surprise," said Jesse. "So go on hunting." He went into his office, looked up the number and called Holden and Wirtz. It was an address on Beverly Boulevard, a very good address. When he penetrated past the receptionist he had a little argument with the secretary, who told him that Mr. Holden had appointments scheduled all afternoon, and wanted to know chapter and verse about Jesse's business with him. Jesse was pa-

tient, an important matter involving one of Mr. Holden's clients,
and at last she said she could fit him in for a brief appointment
at four-thirty.

He had a couple of appointments himself, and one of them
was with a client who had a new will in mind. It turned out to
be rather a complicated one, and he only got rid of the man at
four o'clock. It wasn't raining today but was gray and cold, and
traffic was slow across town; he found the address, a new high-
rise far out on Beverly, with underground parking. A leisurely
elevator carried him to the eleventh floor; the Holden and Wirtz
offices were at the front of the building, and a slick blond receptionist told him that he was ten minutes late, she'd see if Mr.
Holden was free. Eventually he was showed in to a handsomely
appointed paneled office with a large mahogany desk and deep
leather chairs.

Holden stood up politely, a tall good-looking man in his mid-
fifties with thinning gray hair, glasses, sharp tailoring, wary eyes.
He offered Jesse a chair. "And what can we do for you, Mr.
Falkenstein?"

"About Mrs. Ruth Traxler," said Jesse. "I'm representing her
niece, Mrs. Charlene Garland. Mrs. Garland felt she should have
some legal advice about—umm—the situation in general. After
what she told me, I was rather surprised at your reported attitude, Mr. Holden. I don't suppose you swallowed Mr. Jerry
Smith's interesting little story as wholesale as your client has. Or
what do you think about it?"

"That." Holden regarded him with a taut little smile. "I see.
Of course one takes your client's point. Yes, I know all about it
—Mrs. Traxler came to me almost at once the—er—young man
appeared on the scene. It's a difficult position."

"But not," said Jesse gently, "very complicated."

"I hope you're not implying any veniality on our part," said
Holden smugly. "Mrs. Traxler can be a difficult woman to deal
with. I suppose it's possible that the young man is her son, by
what he says—oh, she brought him to see me—"

"When she wanted to make a new will? He showed up a couple of months ago, I understand." Holden wouldn't tell him anything about a will, of course; the client's private business.

Holden said pleasantly, "You know better than to ask that, Mr. Falkenstein. I must say the young man impressed me as quite straightforward, but in any case, as lawyers we have to look at the realities of the legal position, don't we? There's quite evidently no way of resolving the position with any certainty. He was quite frank—he grew up in a Methodist orphanage for boys at Long Beach, he was taken there by a minister after he was found abandoned, and the authorities never were able to trace his origin, that's all he knows. It was, as far as he does know, several months after the kidnapping. And that leaves it entirely up in the air, there's no proof one way or the other. And I needn't tell you that Mrs. Traxler is absolutely convinced that he is her son." Holden shrugged. "There's no arguing with an obstinate woman."

"You're her trustees. You're not concerned to see her victimized by a crook?"

"Is he?" asked Holden. "There's no evidence, you know. He could be what she thinks he is. Perhaps it's a remote possibility, but it could be." Suddenly he unbent slightly, facing Jesse across the expensive mahogany; he brought out a briar pipe and began to fill it, and he gave Jesse a half smile. "I ask you, Falkenstein, what the hell could Bob Wirtz or I do about it? The fellow wouldn't have been so frank on all that if he knew we could poke any holes in it. I've written to the directors of that orphanage, and I haven't any doubt they'll back up his story. Which leaves us where? Nowhere."

"There's no possibility the child's fingerprints are on record from the investigation at that time?"

"No," said Holden. "That came up at the time a body was found—the FBI hadn't been able to get any prints at the house. And there weren't any birthmarks, anything as convenient as that"—his smile was wintry—"if that had occurred to you. There were only a few photographs, and a child of five—a man of twenty-six—" He shrugged again. "The operative point is, nobody will ever convince Mrs. Traxler he isn't her son, and lacking proof one way or the other—we have to deal with realities, Mr. Falkenstein. I'm frank to tell you, if there'd been other children, any closer relatives, there might be reason to—but what the hell could we do about it, I ask you?"

"No proof one way or the other," said Jesse.

"Exactly, you see the position. I'm bound to say," said Holden thoughtfully, "I'm just as glad Halliday isn't here to see it—it would have worried him like hell, he was a personal friend. As it is—"

"Yes," said Jesse, "you have to deal with the woman, and it'd be even more difficult if you riled her, is what you're saying. I can see that. And you say, nothing to prove her wrong. Had it occurred to you that all this convincing info he fed her could have been passed on to him by somebody? Some servant, a former servant, former friend—anybody who knew it."

"Possible," said Holden, "but there'd be no way to show any connection, would there? I should imagine over twenty-one years she's had a succession of servants and talked to a great many people—she's quite a talker, Mr. Falkenstein. But the bottom line is, you'd never convince her he's not her own darling boy, miraculously returned to her. I quite see your client's point of view, but there it is."

Jesse stood up. "Well, that's your point of view, Mr. Holden. There could be other ways to look at it." He reflected, riding down in the slow elevator, that Holden and Wirtz would be a busy firm, doubtless with the handling of other trusts and all sorts of business for important clients; the Traxler estate, probably to be wound up in the next few years, wouldn't be one of such great concern to them. The woman just another client, not a personal friend; probably neither of them had known Traxler personally at all. He wondered academically what the estate consisted of. The original business had been sold, Charlene Garland had said. If he knew Holden and Wirtz, there would be some solid, sound investments, but it might well be one of their less important accounts. Holden wasn't the man to go chasing wild geese, waste time where he couldn't see any benefit.

It had begun to rain again and it was after five. He started home through heavy traffic; he had to be in court in the morning on another divorce settlement, and he had an afternoon of appointments.

*　*　*

He didn't get to the office until after lunch, and Jimmy said as he came in, "We finally tracked down that Gilchrist, he's at the Holiday Inn right here in Hollywood."

"Good," said Jesse. "I'd better talk to him myself." He had half an hour before the first client of the day, and put the call through, but Gilchrist wasn't in. He wondered absently what Gilchrist was doing here. Research, on what?

Two of the clients wanted to make wills and one had a damage suit in mind; that took up most of the afternoon. But he did a little more thinking about the Traxler thing on his way home. He didn't often discuss clients with Nell, but he knew she'd be interested in this one and told her about it over dinner.

Nell was indignant. "It's like vultures," she said. "Preying on that poor silly woman. And you know, Jesse, what the Garland woman said, she'd probably have left her something, she seemed to be fair about the money being her husband's, but now there's been a fight that man might get everything. It's criminal. There must be some way to show he couldn't possibly be the son—"

Jesse said ruminatively, "If I'm reading between lines right, she's already made a new will. If it was before the row with Charlene, she may be making another. Holden wouldn't tell me about that, but he's right that it all seems to be up in the air, and unless you could offer her some concrete proof she'd never believe it. Been thinking where it'd be likeliest there might be some concrete proof. Where would be the likeliest source for all that information, you know."

"The servants," said Nell. "It's queer to think of anybody having live-in servants these days—but that's because we're just ordinary people. Somebody who was working for them when the kidnapping happened—or has worked for her since. Somebody who knew she might be—easy to convince. Somebody who knew this Smith—but that seems farfetched too, Smith having such a convenient background to play the part—"

"When you think about it," said Jesse, "there are all sorts of possibilities. That orphanage—Holden starting a desultory look there, at least doing that much, but he's right—Smith wouldn't have been as open about that if there was anything damaging to find out there, to say he couldn't be the Traxler boy. The servants—" He passed over his cup for a refill of coffee. "Where do people like the Traxlers get servants? Private employment agency? Wonder if Mrs. Garland would know. This Gilchrist had an interview before he wrote up the account in that book, and I'll bet she came out with all that to him, showed him the carefully preserved nursery."

"That," said Nell, "is morbid, all right. A terrible thing, losing a child that way—well, anyway, never to know what really happened—you wouldn't forget it, but to keep on dwelling on it, brooding over the toys and clothes—"

"And that," said Jesse, "making it all the likelier she'd be ripe for the con game. Anybody who knew that—"

"I suppose so. But, Jesse, even if you found the somebody who might have given him all that information, there might not be any way to prove it. Nobody would admit it—it'd amount to some kind of criminal charge, wouldn't it?"

"Conspiracy to obtain money by fraudulent means—words to that effect. Yes. I'd like to talk to those servants—old and new—like to have a look at Mr. Smith for myself. But there's another possibility. The FBI doesn't publicize everything it knows. They must have come up with something on that kidnapping, even when they never got anybody for it. And it's a little odd that that body couldn't be positively identified—the forensic scientists were pretty damned smart and had all sorts of investigative tools even twenty years ago. Damn it, the FBI's just as close-mouthed to a civilian lawyer just trying to do his best for a client, but maybe when they know it might mean a felony charge on somebody they'd open up. Can but try to persuade somebody to talk about it."

He wandered down to his den while Nell cleaned up the

kitchen; the baby was long in bed, and Athelstane somnolent in front of the fireplace. At nine o'clock he tried that Holiday Inn again, and this time got James Gilchrist. Gilchrist disappointed him slightly. The voice on the phone was a pleasant baritone, friendly and frank. "Well, I'm fairly busy, Mr. Falkenstein, what did you want to see me about?"

"I won't take up an hour of your time, Mr. Gilchrist." He'd prefer to see the man in person. "Say nine tomorrow morning? I could meet you where you're staying if that's convenient."

"Oh, I suppose so—all right, nine tomorrow."

* * *

At first sight Jesse was even more disappointed with Gilchrist. Gilchrist was tall and lanky as Jesse himself, and a good deal better looking, with a shock of curly brown hair just sprinkled with gray and a square-jawed nearly handsome face with quick, friendly brown eyes. He gave Jesse a firm handclasp, looking at him curiously, and stood back to let him into the motel room. Apart from an open suitcase and a little litter on the dresser top, the room was neat and clean.

"So what's your business with me? You're a lawyer, you said. I don't know anybody out here except a fellow at the *Times,* we used to be on the same paper in New York years back."

Jesse took the one armchair and laid *Unsolved Mysteries* on his lap. "I'll tell you, it seems to be connected to this book of yours," and he gave Gilchrist a brief rundown. Gilchrist, sitting on the bed chain smoking, interrupted with a few surprised expletives.

"That's the damndest thing I ever heard, Mr. Falkenstein. My God, you think my write-up triggered it, gave somebody the idea?"

"I think somebody used it, Mr. Gilchrist. I understand you had an interview with Mrs. Traxler at the time you wrote this?"

"I did," said Gilchrist equably.

"How did you go about writing it up, did you talk to any of the FBI agents on the case, or—"

"Not much," said Gilchrist. "They wouldn't give me the time

of day—well, they're busy men and they've got rules and regulations—not supposed to talk about cases to civilians. I did find
out that a couple of the Feds who were on the case are retired
now, but I didn't follow up that angle. I wasn't doing an in-
depth study of it, you know—any of those cases. That"—he ges-
tured at *Unsolved Mysteries*—"is just the popular slick job, call
it a potboiler if you like—it sells. I was covering a good many
cases, you can see for yourself—I just hit the highlights. Actually, I didn't have to do a hell of a lot of research. I'd done all I
had to do on the cases back East, and I hit Chicago on the Crater thing, but that's been written up so often you could get all
the relevant facts at any library. I'd only come to California to
get some original information on the Black Dahlia killing, and
that was a washout, every police officer who worked that one is
dead. It was nearly forty years ago, after all, and everything I
got on it was from the morgue at the L.A. *Times*. To tell you
the truth, I'd never heard of this Traxler snatch, I suppose it
made the second pages a few times on city papers back East,
but I didn't remember it. I came across it down at the morgue
and followed it up—I needed a couple more cases to pad the
book, and it was just the kind of thing I could use. I got most of
it from what had been in the *Times*. Talked to a couple of the
Feds, none who'd been on it, but I didn't get much from them as
I say." Gilchrist cocked his head at him. "My God, this thing
you're telling me about—if it is a con game, were you thinking I
could be the co-conspirator briefing the con man? Not guilty."

"Did you know enough, Mr. Gilchrist?"

He considered. "Well, the Traxler woman talked—she didn't
need any prompting. Very autocratic old lady, very aristocratic,
but I thought she was just damned pathetic. Hanging onto old
griefs. Oh, she talked and talked. I hadn't really expected much
from the interview, but all that about never believing her darling boy was dead, a mother would know in her heart and so on,
was just what the public eats up. Yes, she showed me the nursery, the toys, the clothes—" He stabbed out his latest cigarette.
"Like probing the aching tooth, senseless, that kind of thing. I
think I recall her mentioning what he'd called a big stuffed bear,

Huggy or something like that—I don't remember the rocking horse or about the nurse's pet name, any of the rest of that."

"Yes," said Jesse. "And what are you doing out here again, Mr. Gilchrist, if you don't mind my asking?"

"Research on another book," said Gilchrist promptly. "More popular stuff. Free-lancing beats the hell out of trying to make deadlines on the morning edition, and I got damned tired of editors telling me which way to slant stories. We haven't come up with a title yet, but this one is all about modern police forces and the latest investigative techniques. I've spent some time with the boys in New York, Pittsburgh, Philly, Chicago—with all the flak they get elsewhere they're always grateful for a sympathetic writer. Of course, the force here is supposed to be the tops anywhere, and I must say the Chief was very man-to-man, gave me fifteen minutes and a letter asking all his underlings to treat me pretty and cooperate. Very helpful."

"I see," said Jesse absently. "Well, I could give you a couple of personal introductions—my brother-in-law is with the Hollywood Division."

"God, that'd be great," said Gilchrist. "I'd be very grateful, Mr. Falkenstein. They're all so damned busy, the crime rate what it is, they tend to brush me off and say come back later. I'm afraid I couldn't help you at all about this Traxler thing. That's a wild one. Er—would you have time to make that introduction now, by any chance?" He looked eager.

Slightly amused, Jesse agreed. It was more or less on his way to the office. Gilchrist trailed him across town to the new station house on Fountain, and Jesse took him in and introduced him to Clock, who was swearing over typing a report and acknowledged the introduction testily.

"I was just wondering, Andrew, about your original reports on that snatch—while you boys were on it, before the Feds got called in. Would they still be kicking around somewhere, maybe on microfilm?"

"Are you kidding?" asked Clock. "Twenty-one years, and we've moved to the new building since."

"Yes, that's what I was afraid of. Don't suppose there'd be

much in them anyway. I'd better get down to my own office."
He left Gilchrist sitting beside Clock's desk taking rapid shorthand notes, presumably on the layout of the big communal detective office. He had a fairly busy day ahead.

When he got to the office, Jean told him, "You just had a call
from a duchess. Veddy, veddy British and autocratic. That Mrs.
Traxler."

"Oh?" said Jesse.

"She just had your letter. The postal service gets worse and
worse. She doesn't quite understand what Mr. Falkenstein
wishes to discuss with her, but she's agreeable to see you to
make her position quite clear, to her niece's satisfaction. She'll
be pleased to receive you at ten A.M. tomorrow."

"Oh, really," said Jesse. "Good thing I haven't any appointments in the morning. Or have I?"

"You're free until one o'clock," said Jean dryly.

*　*　*

It was a humdrum, boring day, with six tedious, long-winded
clients and more rain slithering down the windows. He was just
late enough starting home that he got snarled in the worst of the
rush-hour traffic, and arrived at the house on Paradise Lane
tired and annoyed with his job. Nell was soothing and shep-
herded Davy off with the excuse that Daddy was too tired to
read to him now; maybe before bed. Jesse built himself a much
needed bourbon and water and began to relax in front of the
fire. Nell brought him a bowl of pretzels and Athelstane, galva-
nized into interest, came to sit on his feet and beg.

"Don't you give him more than a couple. He's overweight
now. Do you want roquefort or blue cheese on the salad?"

"Either one. I'm just glad to be home."

But after the drink and dinner he felt better. He gave
Charlene Garland theoretical time for her own dinner and
looked up her number at eight-thirty. She lived in West Hollywood.

A girl's light, pleasant voice answered the phone, said politely,
"Just a minute, please," and he heard her calling her mother. She

sounded like a nice girl. Probably Charlene Garland's family was a nice one, the children well brought up. And she'd known trouble, losing her husband so young. It would be just more bad luck, and a damned shame, if all Uncle Tom's money should be given away to a smooth con man—just because there had been a little boy lost twenty-one years ago.

"Oh, Mr. Falkenstein," said her slightly throaty contralto voice. "Have there been any—developments?"

"Well, I've got an appointment to meet your aunt tomorrow morning."

"No! I'll be interested to hear how that turns out, but I don't really expect you'll be able to bring about any reconciliation. She isn't loving me very much. I wasn't very polite to her—I lost my temper, as I told you. The idea of that—that *actor* battening on her and probably coming in for all the money—"

"I hope to meet him too. But I wanted to ask you something."

"Yes, of course."

"Do you have any idea where your aunt would get her servants? An employment agency?"

"Goodness, I don't—wait a minute. Yes, I just barely remember her mentioning—the man she had before this one, she had to fire him. He was always getting drunk. That was a year or so ago, I think, around there. We were there to dinner one night when she mentioned it, and she said this agency, Miss Somebody's agency—was usually reliable, she'd certainly give them a piece of her mind for sending her such a fellow. Miss—Miss—it was an Irish name, Mc something—McRory—McGrory—McGraw, I think that was it, McGraw. I haven't any idea where it is."

"Do you know anything about the servants she had when the kidnapping happened?"

"I could tell you something—not much. There was a couple, man and wife, Mr. and Mrs. Dillon, I think the name was. They were nice, she'd had them for several years, since before Tommy was born. Mrs. Dillon was the cook and housekeeper—she was a heavenly cook, you never tasted anything like her pastry—and he looked after the car and drove Aunt Ruth and did odd jobs around the house. Looking back, I suppose it was a wonderfully easy job for them, not much work to do really, because there was a full-time maid—she didn't live in—and Uncle Tom always drove himself. Why do you want to know? Oh, I see, they'd have known—all that. But the Dillons were nice people, Mr. Falkenstein."

"When did they leave?"

"I don't know. I told you Bob and I were up in Fresno when the kidnapping happened, and afterward. When we came back here, there were new servants—well, naturally the nursemaid had gone. And there are different ones now."

"Yes. You said something about a cleaning service?"

"One of the commercial companies, they come in on a regular basis, however often you want them, once a month or whatever. To do the basic jobs—floors and windows and walls and ceilings. It must be nice to have that kind of money," she said without rancor. "I don't know, but I suppose they employ quite a few people, it wouldn't be the same ones every time."

"What about the servants there now?"

"I don't know much about them. She never had a married couple after the Dillons. She's got a cook—excuse me, she's a cook-housekeeper, I think her name is Goodman or Goodis, something like that, she's the only live-in servant there now. Well, except for the chauffeur-handyman. I don't know when they did that, but I expect after the Dillons left Uncle Tom thought it would be more convenient, they had a little two-room apartment built over the garage, for the chauffeur. She's just got the housekeeper and chauffeur now—*just*—it sounds like an English novel, doesn't it? I don't know anything about him at all. I told you she doesn't entertain the way she used to. You know, Mr. Falkenstein, I've been thinking about it, and of course she's a fool, but you can understand her—why she's doing it. She hadn't anything left, after Tommy—and Uncle Tom. About all she ever had was the money, and it was—it wasn't a life with any meaning. Dinner parties, and afternoon tea, and shopping, and the bridge club. There wasn't anything to it. And Uncle Tom wasn't one for going out much, he liked to read. And after he sold the business—after Tommy was gone—he hadn't anything either. I told you how he just lost interest in everything."

"Yes. Yes, it's understandable in a way. So Solomon says, *the way of a fool is right in his own eyes.*"

"Not that it makes me feel any better about it. What do you think—about it?" She didn't mean Mrs. Traxler's foolishness.

"One thing I think is that Holden and Wirtz may have a slightly undeserved reputation for reliability," said Jesse.

"I didn't like Mr. Holden. I'd never met him before, of course. No reason to. But I didn't like him."

"I don't think I like him much, either. Part of normal legal ethics, you do your damndest for the client. Within bounds of ethics, so to speak. I see his point of view, but I think he could take a little more interest in his job. Well, I'll let you know what comes of my interview with Mrs. Traxler. Thanks very much."

* * *

Since that photograph of the Traxler house had been taken, probably by a *Times* reporter, all those years ago, the date palms and flowering shrubbery had grown and spread out considerably. In the photograph, the house had looked rather stark and new. This very exclusive and expensive residential area, in the hills above Hollywood, boasted wide lots and many opulent homes. The Traxler house must have been among those first built here when this section of the Hollywood Hills was first subdivided for building, twenty-five or twenty-six years ago. It was a two-story Spanish stucco house with a red-tiled roof; it sat at the top of a rather steep little hill, with a luxuriant spread of green lawn on three sides of it, sloping to the narrow street. There was a flight of shallow cement steps curving up to the square front porch and double doors. The driveway curved up on one side; the garage was hidden behind the house. The street curved too, so that although there were houses at each side of this one, they seemed remote, farther away than they actually were.

Jesse left the Mercedes at the curb and took the steps easily; it was a little climb. He pushed the bell beside the double doors and couldn't hear the chime inside. In forty seconds the right side of the doors opened and he faced a tall, stout, middle-aged woman in a neat housedress. She had a Scandinavian look about her, a rather flat face with high cheekbones and shallow gray eyes. Jesse told her his name. "I think Mrs. Traxler is expecting me."

"Yes, sir," she said stolidly. "Come in, sir. Madam told me you'd be coming. This way, sir."

The wide entry hall was red-tiled with a single walnut table and chair inside the door. She led him ten feet down to a door on the left, opened it and stood back. "It's the gentleman you're expecting, madam."

The living room was unexpectedly large, square and high-ceilinged. It was furnished elegantly but not ostentatiously, in quiet conventional taste, perhaps a little stodgy and old-fashioned. There was a low fire in the hearth, which rose to a black-marble mantel. His hostess sat in one of a pair of large armchairs flanking the hearth. "Mr. Falkenstein," she said, inclining her head stiffly. "Come in." She looked her age, but the iron-gray hair was beautifully and professionally waved, the thin lined face delicately made up, and the plain mauve silk dress might be an original model. She was a handsome old woman rather than once pretty, with a long high-bridged nose and watchful faded blue eyes. She wore two diamond rings and a diamond watch, no other jewelry. "Do sit down," she said. "I'd like to introduce you to my son, Mr. Traxler."

Jesse looked at the erstwhile Jerry Smith as he rose from the other chair, extending a hand. "I'm pleased to meet you, sir." The hand was firm and slightly moist.

Charlene Garland had said, a smooth actor, and he could be all of that. But for some reason Jesse felt a little surprised: Mr. Smith was something more and something less than he had expected. He was stockily built, not overly tall, with very blond hair cut smoothly short, and without being overtly handsome he gave the impression of appealing boyish good looks, with a wide mobile mouth, very blue eyes and a slightly tanned face. He sat down again, and at her gesture Jesse took a third chair drawn up between the pair.

"Do smoke if you like," she said. "There's an ashtray on the table beside you. I agreed to see you, Mr. Falkenstein, because I feel it is only fair to Charlene to make the position perfectly clear." He wondered how hard she worked to preserve the accent, the distinctly British, upper-class accent, clipped and precise; or perhaps it was second nature to her by now. "I must say I was astonished that Charlene should take such a step as to employ a lawyer on a private family matter."

"Well, that's just the question, Mrs. Traxler," he said mildly. "Is it a family matter?"

"You come to the point, sir. Perhaps it shouldn't surprise me that Charlene found someone of your caliber." It was not a calculated insult, but cutting judgment.

"Now—" said the other man. "Mr. Falkenstein, I don't want you to think—"

"Tommy," she said. "I will handle this matter. You need not say anything at all. I am, of course, well aware that Charlene refuses to accept the fact that this is my son." Her eyes went to the other man and softened. "But I am the best judge of that—I am the one who would know, and he has given me quite adequate proof of his identity. There is simply no more to be said about that."

"Er—Mother—"

"I said I will handle this affair, Tommy. There is nothing more to be said," she repeated emphatically. "You may tell Charlene that I am quite prepared to treat her as one of my family if she will behave herself and stop acting like a spoiled and jealous child. I dare say I could be forgiven for never wishing to see her again, after the wild and insulting things she has said to me. But if she likes to call and apologize, I am willing to excuse her behavior. If not, I'm afraid she must put up with the consequences."

"And what," asked Jesse meekly, "are the consequences, Mrs. Traxler?"

She said sharply, "I can hardly suppose that either you or my niece need to have the matter spelled out, sir. I really do not understand why she consulted a lawyer at all—there is no legal action whatever to be taken. I only agreed to see you, Mr. Falkenstein, to give you that message for her." The other man cleared his throat and as if anticipating interruption she said instantly, "Tommy, you needn't add anything to that."

He gave Jesse a mutely deprecatory glance. "I only thought—"

"It is purely a family matter, and as long as Charlene understands that clearly, she may make her own choice as to how she intends to behave. And I think that is all there is to say." Suddenly she stood up; she was taller than he had expected. "Good morning, Mr. Falkenstein." The interview was at an end.

And as he walked down the curving flight of shallow steps, unwillingly he found himself admiring the old girl. An obstinate, silly, sentimental and fairly stupid old woman, but a foolishly gallant one, going her own way. And—he could agree with Gilchrist—pathetic.

And what could you make of Mr. Smith? A curiously amorphous, unplaceable personality. Jerry Smith, from the religious orphanage—and where since? And with whom since?

He sat at his desk and thought about Mr. Smith. Presently he hunted up the few notes he'd taken during his first interview with Charlene Garland and found the name of her employers. He got handed around a little, eventually got her. "I'm sorry to call you at work—"

"That's all right. What did you think of Aunt Ruth? Did you meet him?"

"Oh, yes. I'm not sure what I think. Mrs. Garland, I'd like you to write down everything you remember about that letter he wrote your aunt. You saw it, read it. And everything you remember about what he told her afterward."

"All the evidence that convinced her, in other words. I put down some of it, before I came to see you. Yes, I'll do that. I don't think I'd miss anything—it's the sort of thing you wouldn't forget. I'll do it right away. What *did* you think of him?"

"Not quite what I expected somehow. He's—plausible."

"Oh, I'll grant you that!" she laughed. "What are you going to do now? Do you have any ideas about it?"

"Clients always want action to justify the retainer. I'll be thinking about it, Mrs. Garland."

* * *

It was Friday night, and the Falkensteins were going out to dinner with their in-laws. They had discovered a reliable teenage girl living two blocks down the hill who was usually available as a baby-sitter, and Davy reluctantly accepted her; they didn't leave him all that often.

They got to the Clocks' house in Hollywood at six-forty-five, and without question proceeded first to the nursery to renew acquaintance with the youngest member of the family. She was very young indeed, having just celebrated her second month in the world. She had turned out to be Elaine Amanda because Fran had belatedly realized the dangers of nicknames. "If it was Amanda," she'd said, "I know in my bones as soon as she started school she'd be Mandy, which is just too, too Old South. And Elaine is nicer anyway—more dignified." The very new Miss Clock was a rather dignified baby, not given to yelling at unseemly hours. She had come equipped with Fran's black hair and cornflower-blue eyes, and she stared up at them dreamily, waving pink starfish hands.

"She is a darling," said Nell. "I'd like a girl now. As soon as Davy isn't quite such a handful—"

"I told you," said Clock fatuously, "both of them getting prettier every day."

"But we'd better have dinner early," said Fran. "She's due to nurse again by eight o'clock, and she may look serene enough now, but she'll let us know loud and clear. Andrew, you get Jesse a drink—sherry for Nell and me." The hairy black Peke, Sally, trotted after them into the living room, but she had much better manners than Athelstane and never begged for handouts.

And over dinner Clock said, "You had to wish Gilchrist on me. He's been tagging after us like a faithful hound. Oh, I don't mind—he's a nice fellow, and he does have that letter from the

Chief." He yawned over a second cup of coffee. "It's just, I'm fairly beat. It's been one thing after another—the rate usually goes up in hot weather, but this last couple of weeks it's been murder. There's this damned anonymous body—well, see what that address turns up—and a double homicide at a movie house of all unlikely things, and that goddamned spate of forged checks—all the damned paper work—and the usual heists—"

"Don't bring the office home, darling," said Fran.

"No, sorry. I told Gilchrist, he's looking for examples of super-modern investigative techniques, he'd better talk to the lab men at SID downtown. The average caper plainclothes harness men are looking at is just as crude and simple"—he yawned again—"as Cain versus Abel. Which reminds me, Jesse, what about your interesting con man? You have any further inspiration on that?"

"I don't know," said Jesse dissatisfiedly. "Maybe not so simple as your average heist man, Andrew, but just as much up in the air."

3

Saturday started out to be a frustrating day. Jesse got to the FBI office in Hollywood at nine o'clock and talked to a man in the outer office. All the Feds seemed to look the same, whatever the size or shape or age: bland, polite fellows in impeccable business suits, with noncommittal voices and eyes and manners.

"I'm afraid there's nobody here at the moment who could spend any time with you, when the matter is not urgent, Mr. Falkenstein." The man at the desk, by the name sign, was a Robert Upjohn, thirtyish, bland, courteous. "Perhaps Monday or Tuesday—several of our regular agents are in Washington at the moment. I think Mr. Bradshaw could probably give you some time on Monday." It was polite but definite, nothing to do but thank him and go away.

Jesse went away to a public phone booth and started to look up employment agencies. After a little hunt he found what he was looking for, an E. McGraw Employment Agency, specializing in experienced domestic help, at an address on Sunset Boulevard in Beverly Hills.

At least it wasn't raining. He drove out there, and discovered, as he might have expected, that it was closed on Saturday. It was just a hole-in-the-wall small office, upstairs in an old but well-maintained office building.

He sat in the car and ruminated. He hadn't taken much of a

retainer from Charlene Garland, and since she hadn't all the money in the world, she wouldn't thank him for running up the bill, but if there was anything definite to be got here on this thing, anything significant to find out, maybe some judicious outlay would be well spent.

He drove back to Hollywood, turned down Fairfax Avenue, and found a slot in a public parking lot half a block down from the building he wanted, a rather shabby old four-story building. He climbed stairs to the second floor, and went down the hall to a glass-fronted door bearing the legend THOMAS GARRETT ASSO-CIATES, PRIVATE INVESTIGATIONS.

Evidently business was slow; he got taken in by the receptionist at once, to Garrett's private office. "And what can we do for you, Mr. Falkenstein?" asked Garrett genially. He was a big, broad man with a bald head and cynical eyes.

Jesse sat down in the chair beside the littered desk and accepted a cigarette and embarked on his tale. "You can see it's a distinct possibility," he said, when he'd covered that, "that the source of the information could be the servants. I'd like a little run down on them."

"Sure," said Garrett interestedly. "We can do that for you. Question of catching them on days off, easiest approach—have a look at their associates and so on. They live in? That makes it a littler harder, but we can do something. I've got Allen free, and a couple of other operatives. I suppose it'd also occurred to you, servants past and present?"

"Oh, yes," said Jesse wryly. "We'll have to go into that too, if I can get anything at all from that employment agency. If possible, I'd like to find out something about their attitudes to Mrs. Traxler—" He emitted a column of smoke thoughtfully. "Don't somehow feel she's the kind of woman to inspire any deep loyalty in her servants, they won't be the old family-retainer types."

"I get you," said Garrett, massaging his jaw. "That makes it a little tougher, something more than having a look at neighbors and associates. The housekeeper—I've got a pretty smart girl on tab, Mary Lester. I can turn her loose on the housekeeper and see what she comes up with. The chauffeur—my God, these moneyed types—he ought to be fairly easy."

"It's your job," said Jesse. "You know how to do it. Just don't go throwing expenses around too hot and heavy."

"We'll do our best for you. Don't expect anything right away."

"I know, I know. But there's also Mr. Smith. I could bear to know what he does and where he goes outside that house."

"Yeah, the principal," said Garrett. "That's an interesting little caper, Mr. Falkenstein. That should be easier—question of shadowing him around. He won't be dancing attendance on the old lady twenty-four hours a day."

"I understand she's provided him with his own car, probably a regular allowance. He'll be getting around, enjoying himself however he pleases—within reason. He's got to keep her sweet, we can guess. No undesirable riffraff friends, no sleazy bars. But I could bear to know if he has any friends around about, who they are. He grew up in Long Beach, but he'll have been away from that orphanage a good long time—I've got no idea where he's been since, what doing, what jobs he might have had, who he's associated with. Don't know what he was doing up to when he contacted Mrs. Traxler. He must have been earning a living somehow." He ruminated. "It's a very long chance he has a police record anywhere, but it might be useful if you can contrive to get his prints. I might get Andrew to run them through records."

Garrett shook his head. "That wouldn't be so easy. But we can have a good look at him at a little distance. I think I'll let Allen take him, he blends into any background."

Jesse stood up. "Well, I'd like anything you can get as soon as possible."

"Sure. We ought to turn up a little something by sometime next week, if there's anything there to get. I'll be in touch, let you know. You can leave a retainer with the girl."

❋   ❋   ❋

At noon on Saturday, Clock sat back and swore as he finished typing a report. He said, "Talk about thankless jobs." He grinned at Gilchrist, the only other occupant of the big office, and added, "I feel like goofing off this afternoon. That thing of Jesse's—it's a hell of lot more interesting than anything we're working—none of my business but maybe we can help him out a little. Maybe give you something you can use too, Gilchrist, if you'd be interested. What do you say we go and call on Sergeant Rector and see if he remembers anything about that snatch?"

"Sure," said Gilchrist.

"He put in about forty years at the thankless job, he could tell you something about the old days—contrast between the way we had to work back then before we had all the modern gadgets down at the lab." He looked at his watch. "Tell you what, Pete ought to be back with whatever he got at that address any minute, and then we'll take off for lunch. I just hope to God nothing new goes down. If we could get that damned body identified—and there'll be all those damned potential witnesses to locate and talk to on that other homicide, and not one goddamned thing in it—making bricks without straw." He rubbed his prognathous jaw, looking disgusted. "And all the heisters—but hell, there are enough boys around to mind the store for a couple of hours. I may not deserve a break, but I think I'll take one anyway."

"You might get her identified by prints eventually," said Gilchrist.

"Maybe," said Clock, yawning. "I hate these damned things all up in the air."

The unidentified body was that of a red-haired young woman found sprawled along the curb of a quiet residential street up in the hills off Outpost Drive. All her clothes bore anonymous labels of national brands, and the few pieces of costume jewelry she was wearing were just as anonymous. She had probably been manually strangled; there hadn't been an autopsy report yet. The double homicide posed a lot more work, both paper work and legwork; a young couple knifed to death in the back row of a porn movie house on Thursday night, found when the place closed down at 2:00 A.M. They had both carried identification—Wilma Taylor and Joe Lopez; this and that had emerged about them. The ticket seller remembered them coming in about nine o'clock, they'd been regular patrons, and the first show was over at about eleven, so probably they'd been killed before then. Taylor had been a waitress at a restaurant on La Cienega, Lopez had worked at a garage. A couple of her friends had said she had been going steady with Joe for about three months, but she'd had a lot of different boyfriends, it could have been somebody she'd thrown over, somebody jealous; nobody so far could name one like that. The back rows weren't always filled up, and if somebody had gone in and sat alongside them, in the dark, who would have noticed? But they'd have to try to track down the people who'd been sitting nearest, and that would be an exercise in futility. If anybody had heard a little disturbance at any time, not much notice would have been taken, in a place like that.

Petrovsky came in looking disgruntled and said, "Dead end."

"Who lives there?" asked Clock. The only thing of any possible interest on the red-haired girl, in one pocket of her coat, had been a business card from a restaurant in Henderson, Nevada, with an address scrawled on the back: Miramar Apartments, Apartment D, LA. That was an address on Eleventh Street downtown.

"An old fellow by the name of Robert Dunne," said Petrovsky. "He's about sixty-five and he broke his hip a while back, gets around in a walker. He hasn't been able to drive since then, he's thinking of selling his car. He lives alone, he's a bachelor. I don't see him having anything to do with the redhead. But the manager says a young fellow just moved out of apartment C, and you know, Andrew, that scrawl—it could be C instead of D, you look at it twice. All the manager knows is his name, Jeff Gerard, he'd lived there about six months, nice quiet tenant, always on time with the rent, no noisy parties. She didn't know where he worked, and she can't even give a good description—he was sort of medium, brown hair, kind of thin, just an ordinary young fellow."

"Hell," said Clock, without emphasis. "I'm taking the afternoon off, Pete." And he might complain that Jesse had saddled him with Gilchrist, but he liked Gilchrist, who was an amusing talker and had had varied experiences as a reporter.

They had lunch at the coffee shop on Fountain. Clock had looked up Rector's address; he lived in Glendale. They had a little hunt for the house, at the end of a narrow, dead-end street north in that sprawling suburb, an unpretentious stucco house with lawn and rose bushes in front. A comfortable looking gray-haired woman opened the door and welcomed them in. "Matt will be glad to see anybody from the station—he hasn't near enough to do since he retired, never was one for working around the yard much, or reading. He's down in the den."

They found ex-Sergeant Rector looking bored over a TV talk show; he snapped off the set and greeted Clock in surprise. Clock hadn't known him well; Rector had been down in Juvenile his last ten years on the force, since Clock had been a detective and then made rank. He was a sinewy spare old man, nearly bald, with a lantern jaw. "What brings you here, Sergeant? Oh, glad to see you—always glad to have somebody to talk to—life's kind of boring these days. Sit down."

Clock introduced Gilchrist, and proceeded to tell Rector about the Traxler affair. "Garcia said he thought you were on that snatch, all that time ago. You remember anything about it?"

Rector said thoughtfully, "Now that's the hell of a thing, isn't it? Yeah, something. It was the only snatch I was ever on, and just after I got transferred up to Hollywood. God, that's a while back."

Clock and Gilchrist had sat down on the loveseat across from him; he hitched his chair nearer and shoved the ashtray closer to them on the little coffee table. "Yeah, that thing. We got called out first thing in the morning, they'd just found the kid was missing when the nursemaid got up around seven, I think. Naturally, everybody was in the hell of a tizzy—there were a couple of squads out and when we got there all the men were still looking around the yard, under bushes and so on, in case the kid had just gone out to play—but the father said the front and back doors were still locked, and I don't know why the uniformed men had bothered, once they saw the screen was cut out. One thing I do remember, hell of a thing in a way, see, there was central air conditioning—not all that common then—well, you could see from the house there was money—and it had gone on the fritz a couple of days before. They were supposed to come and fix it in a day or so. If that had been on, all the windows would have been shut and the snatcher'd probably have made enough noise getting the window open to wake up the nurse. Just chance—or maybe the snatcher knew about it." He gave a shrug. "Anyway, it was pretty damned obvious right away it was a snatch—the screen was cut out, we found it in a flower bed underneath the window—and there was a ladder right there leaned against the house, up to the window."

Clock said to Gilchrist, "By your account, that had been out in plain sight for a couple of days—it could have been spotted by somebody."

"That's right," said Gilchrist.

"So somebody could have known there was a ladder available, even if it got moved to the garage—back then, people didn't lock garages automatically. Which could make it look like an amateur job. But somebody knew the right window to the kid's room."

"Yeah," said Rector. "We didn't get much on questioning everybody—the mother and father were too upset to be thinking straight, and the nursemaid was crying all the time—there were some other servants, they didn't sleep upstairs, and they all said they hadn't heard a thing all night. But with the air conditioning out—"

"Fans going," said Gilchrist. "It was a damned hot night—I understand you get some of your worst heat in September—"

"Too true," said Clock.

"Fans going, in the nurse's room and the parents'—their room was at the front of the house, and what was called the nursery suite at the back. So the nurse wouldn't have heard a thing, her room across a bathroom from the kid's—she was sound asleep with the fan on. I wondered when I read about that if the snatcher knew, or if it was just his dumb luck."

"Yeah," said Rector. "Naturally we called out the lab to print the kid's room, the window and so on, but they didn't pick up a thing—just the usual smudges. It's funny how seldom we do pick up good latents—and naturally, even if it was an amateur, he'd have had the sense to wear gloves. About the only real evidence they did spot was a stain on the pillow on the kid's bed, not much, but the lab men took the pillow in—it got analyzed as chloroform, but that was after the Feds got called in and we were off it. You can see what it looked like pretty clear. Reconstruct it, the snatcher got in up the ladder, had a cloth or something all primed with the chloroform to slap over the kid's face —he was just a little kid, only about four—"

"Five," said Gilchrist.

"—and back down the ladder with the kid. He could have had an accomplice waiting in a car or just been on his own. Anyway, we got pulled off when the Feds came in, and that was the same day as far as I remember—it was an obvious snatch, their baby. And you know the Feds, we never heard any more about it. Naturally there wasn't anything in the papers while it was going on—"

Gilchrist said, "No. Even if the rumor got out, from one of the servants or wherever, I will say the press is usually cooperative about sitting on a thing if they're asked. Or told. The first story broke about a week or ten days later." He lit another cigarette. "They had a tap on the phone, and that was how the ransom demand came in. Those days, they didn't have the Voiceprinter, of course—if they'd ever had a good suspect, that might have pinned it down—"

"It's not admissible as court evidence—yet," said Clock.

"Isn't it? I suppose not—the courts will drag their heels on modern inventions. But at least they'd have known who X was. As it was, just a man's voice, telling the father how to deliver the ransom. A hundred thousand in unmarked bills."

"There are ways to mark it so it doesn't show," said Rector.

"I don't know if they did," said Gilchrist. "There wasn't anything about that in the *Times* stories. But one thing struck me, it was a fairly smart idea, how they got hold of the ransom money. The racing season was on, and Traxler was told to take the

money in a briefcase and mingle with the crowd at the pari-mutuel windows at Santa Anita. I take it there'd have been quite a
crowd. I suppose the Feds had men spotted all around, but in all
the confusion somebody was able to grab that briefcase and get
away with it without being nabbed. At least, that was the story
the press got—the Feds might have a different version."

Rector said, "I didn't remember that. I saw the stories in the
paper later. But they never got the kid back."

"No," said Gilchrist, blowing smoke thoughtfully. "No. The
snatcher promised that he'd be returned within twenty-four
hours, nothing was apparently said about how or where, and it
was after there'd been no sign of him by four or five days later
that the Feds broke the story to the press. With photos of the
boy—last desperate effort to try to locate him. And that was it.
Nothing more ever showed on it, in the press. The money never
turned up, not one bill of it—or at least the press didn't know if
it did—"

"Didn't it?" said Clock. "That doesn't sound like an amateur,
you know. Sounds as if the snatcher—single or plural—knew
how to get it laundered, exchanged and sent out of the country.
They'd take a fifty percent loss on it, but it would have been the
hell of a lot safer. And what about that body?"

"I never heard they found any body," said Rector, surprised.

"I can't tell you much about that," said Gilchrist. "There was
just a bare mention in connection with the Traxler case, it was
about six months later. The body turned up in a land-fill area, a
crew doing some work there found it. I gather there wasn't
much left of it, all the doctors could say was that it could have
been about the right age and size for the Traxler kid. It was
male, anyway. But in the meantime, round about the time of the
kidnapping, there'd been another kid reported missing from another area—I don't know much about your suburbs here—a
place called Studio City. That wasn't a snatch, ordinary family I
gather—all the story said, police speculate a pervert could have
enticed him away from the schoolyard. It was another boy about
five. There were only two stories in the *Times* about the body,
and the second one said the coronor's report was inconclusive,

no possible clear identification. I wonder what the Feds thought about it."

"Yes, so do I," said Clock.

"I never heard about that," said Rector. "But hell, that's what happens most of the time in a snatch, the kid ends up dead. Either intentionally or accidentally. That chloroform—I don't suppose it'd take much to put a little kid like that right out. And they dumped the body quick."

"It was evidently buried," said Gilchrist.

"Well, they wouldn't leave it anywhere to be spotted before they could collect the ransom," said Rector reasonably. "But what you were telling me about this con game—that's the damndest—"

"It's got to be a con game, of course," said Gilchrist. "Doesn't it? The snatchers—either they get rid of the kid, or sometimes they do return them—not often, but now and then. They wouldn't have just walked off and left the kid in the street—and if they had, for God's sake, he'd have been identified then."

"That's why it's hard to understand that fool woman swallowing the tale," said Clock. "A kid that age, say they had just left him, he could tell his own name—"

"To the first cop he got reported to," nodded Gilchrist. "I'm Tommy Traxler and I want to go home to Mama and Daddy. More to the point, he'd be able to say, the bad man had black hair and a moustache, or there were two of them and they called each other Al and Joe. Yeah." He emitted a long stream of smoke reflectively. "Unless, of course—and that's a possibility—he'd been kept under drugs, maybe enough to cause a complete loss of memory. But even then, he'd have been identified sooner or later."

"Women!" said Clock. "You'd think she could see that, it's two plus two. But she's believing what she wants to believe, naturally. Well, this is goofing off with a vengeance." He looked at his watch guiltily.

"By all that," said Rector, "there'd never be any definite proof he is or isn't."

Gilchrist stood up with Clock. "It's a sweet con game all right.

You know, I'm doing a kind of slow burn about it, because he had the damn gall to rope me into it, claim it was my innocuous little potboiler brought his memory back all of a sudden. I damned well would like to help Mr. Falkenstein locate some proof on him." And then he gave the other two a quizzical glance. "Of course, there's just a very remote possibility—it'd be the hell of a joke on everybody, wouldn't it, if he really is Tommy Traxler?"

*　*　*

Jesse had to be in court on Monday morning, and didn't get back to the office until nearly noon. The mail had arrived; his twin efficient Gordons could take care of the run-of-the-mill mail, but Jean had left two letters on his desk. One was an invitation to attend a reunion of his university class; he hadn't kept up with any of his fellow students and couldn't have cared less. The other one was from Charlene Garland. It was neatly typed on typewriter-size paper, and looked businesslike. He read it with interest. "Dear Mr. Falkenstein, I have tried to remember everything you asked me, and put it in order for you. The letter my aunt had from Jerry Smith was typed, pretty sloppily too, on plain paper. It was headed with the address of the motel, I can't remember the exact name, Greentrees or Twelve Trees or something like that, and I think it was on Sunset Boulevard. It was in quite good English, with just a couple of spelling errors. He introduced himself and said he wasn't claiming or expecting anything, he didn't—if I remember the way he put it—know the truth himself, but he just thought she might find what he had to say interesting. He told her how he'd been brought up in a Methodist orphanage and never known anything about his family, that he'd been abandoned and brought to the orphanage when he was about five or six, he didn't know his exact age. And that the orphanage had never found out where he came from, who he'd been living with. He said he didn't remember much of anything about where he'd lived before, just that there'd been an Uncle Bernie and Aunt Mae who'd looked after him for a while, but he remembered other things sort of vaguely, all jumbled together, that he'd never thought much about. He said he remembered once he'd had a toy bear he called Huggy, and a rocking horse named Dapple Peter. And a dog, a live dog, named Bonnie, a gold-colored dog with long ears. And sitting on a man's lap and being let to play with a big gold watch, it had a cover and you pressed a button to make it open. But they were just vague memories and didn't seem to mean much until something happened just lately. He'd been living in San Francisco, he had a job there—he didn't say what—and he was at the library one day and happened to pick up this book—he named it. And when he was reading about that Traxler kidnapping and came to the photographs, he said it was just like a door opening in his mind because he knew that house, he recognized it, and he felt as if it was his house, and all of a sudden a lot of different memories came to him all at once, like a flood. He knew that was where he lived, and he remembered the man with the gold watch playing with him and the gold-colored dog, there was a little rhyme the man always said—'Bow wow wow, whose dog art thou—' And he saw a kind of picture of himself reciting little verses too, 'Hickety pickety my black hen'—he had to recite the verses, it was a big room, he had to say the verses for people when they came. And there was a lady by a table with a lot of shiny silver things on it. He remembered another verse about Hector Protector. And he wondered if all that meant anything to her, because he felt they were real memories and he was so sure he knew that house. And he just signed it yours respectfully. The way I told you, it was a clever letter. And she couldn't wait to see him—when she showed the letter to me, she said she knew in her bones he was her own darling Tommy, but that's nonsense of course. But when he came, he said he remembered the living room, he used to stand by the fireplace to recite the verses, but there'd been a different picture over the mantel, it had a wagon and horses in it. It was a reproduction Constable, I remember it, and Aunt Ruth had had the house redecorated since. And as soon as she took him upstairs he said the dog Bonnie used to have her bed on the landing, and in the nursery he said that door went into Judy's room, only there was a bathroom between.

As I told you, he called his nurse Judy because she'd told him stories about Punch and Judy. And he said he remembered what she looked like, she was sort of fat and always wore a big white apron, and she told him stories about when she was a little girl in a place called Barnstaple. And about something she used to read to him about the bells of London Town. All of that's perfectly true, and it was what convinced Aunt Ruth. But, of course, it doesn't amount to real proof. I should say that quite a lot of people would know all that—she's always talked about Tommy a lot—but to be fair I can't imagine anyone who did know deliberately wanting to deceive her. I hope this is of some help to you."

Jesse digested that in detail for the second time, and a new stray thought crossed his mind. The psychics. She had trotted around to the psychics seeking news of her vanished darling boy, and some of them had told her what she wanted to hear, and some hadn't. Well, there were psychics and psychics, good, bad, and indifferent. But the good ones often came up with the truth. It would be interesting to know, if possible, if Charlene remembered which ones, what any of the reliable ones—if any—had told her. But twenty-one years—

He was annoyed that Charlene Garland had picked him at random on this thing. Such a damned nebulous thing, probably nothing definite ever to be got on it. Round and round the mulberry bush—

Another nursery rhyme. And that one about the bells was in Davy's new book. "Gay go up and gay go down/To ring the bells of London Town—Oranges and lemons,/Say the bells of St. Clement's—You owe me ten shillings,/Say the bells of St. Helen's—"

And if those private eyes ran up much of a bill, Charlene Garland was going to be annoyed too. And the client with the damage suit was coming in for a conference at two o'clock, he'd better go over his notes and do some work on that. He put Mr. Smith at the back of his mind and rummaged for his notes.

The client came and went, and he was still ruminating about the damage suit half an hour later, had just finished dictating a

letter to Jean for the proposed defendant—if he could get it settled out of court, it would save everybody's time—when Jimmy
came in and said, "You've got an uninvited visitor. Mr. Traxler
would like to see you if you have time."

"Who? I'll be damned."

"You've got another appointment in forty-five minutes. Shall I
let him in?"

"Bring him in," said Jesse. All his curiosity about Jerry Smith
came flooding back. He stood up.

He came in looking a little diffident, and he made the same
impression on Jesse he'd made the first time, both more and less
what you might expect of a typical con man. He was smartly
dressed in well-tailored sports clothes, all in shades of brown, his
blond hair smooth, his blue eyes anxious. "I'm sorry if I'm inter-
rupting anything, Mr. Falkenstein." Even his pleasant rather
high voice underlined the boyishness. "I don't want to take too
much of your time, but I felt there were a couple of things I
ought to say to you."

"Sit down, won't you?" Jesse reseated himself at his desk,
offering him the client's chair.

The other man sat up stiffly straight in it and gave him a
deprecatory smile. "The old lady was a little rough on you the
other day, Mr. Falkenstein, I was sorry. All of this isn't your
fault. I guess I can understand how Mrs. Garland feels, but she
shouldn't have said all those things to—" He stopped and went
on, "It feels damned queer to say Mother, you know. I'd just like
to apologize—she's always had everything her own way, and she
can take you up sharp. Look"—he leaned forward and his voice
and eyes were frank, his smile ingenuous—"I'd just like to say
this for anything it might be worth to you." He took out a cigarette, lit it with a quick flick of a lighter. "I know Mrs. Garland
thinks I'm—well, a fake, that I fooled the old lady with a lot of
smooth talk, but that's not so. I don't know what Mrs. Garland
told you or how much she knows, but I really do remember a lot
of things—just the way I told the old lady—about that house,
other things, and being a kid there. I *know* it was there—it was
damned funny, how as soon as I saw that picture I started

remembering—it's all true. And I don't want anybody to think I'm taking her for a ride. It's just that—well it's all been damned awkward, if that's a funny word for it. I don't like hanging around doing nothing, I've supported myself since I left the home—"

"Mind telling me at what?" asked Jesse sleepily.

"No, I had to take what I could get, I graduated from high school, but I'm not really qualified for much of a job—I worked at gas stations and so on, I'm a fair mechanic. But I always wanted to get into some kind of office work, or selling—I think I could be pretty good at that. I never had a chance to get to college. Of course, at the home you were out on your own as soon as you turned eighteen and were out of school and could get a job." He was silent and then said, "You see, she got me to move right in with her, and it's been—sort of queer—well it's been damned nice, I can't deny that, to have money and know who I am, have family of my own—but I don't like all of it. I've wanted to get a job, but she won't hear of it, there's no need for me to work—she expects me to spend all the time playing tennis or getting to know all the grandchildren of her friends, the same kind she is, money and big houses—I couldn't do that. Now she wants me to join a country club, damn it, says my—how her husband always kept up his membership, golf's such good exercise. I don't know how to play golf, for God's sake. It feels wrong, not doing anything to earn my keep. But I think I can bring her around some to see how I feel. I—well, I've only met Mrs. Garland once, and I know she doesn't think much of me, but I'd just like her to know that." He smiled more confidently. "She gave you a message for Mrs. Garland—I guess that's mine. And I'd like her to know how I feel about—about the family part too. I don't know if anybody'd understand that."

"Try me," said Jesse gently.

"Well"—he put out his cigarette—"at the home—oh it's a nice home, Mr. Falkenstein, they treated us fine, if it was kind of strict—but you see it's not like a great big impersonal institution. All the rest of the boys there—they knew who they were. If you see what I mean. Lots of them even had relatives—aunts and uncles or grandparents—people to come and see them and bring presents—they were just in the home because their parents were dead or something. But nobody knew about me. I used to think, I could be anybody—I could be Irish or German or anything, nobody was even sure Jerry Smith was my right name. The biggest reason I wrote the old lady that letter, I'd always wondered —and when I saw the picture of that house, and began to remember all those queer things, I thought, I could be that kid —I could really have somebody I belonged to, family. I didn't think—how it might turn out."

"But you think you can argue her around to let you take a job?"

"Well, about that—she wouldn't hear of my taking the kind of job I've always had, all I'm qualified for. But what I thought I could do, I think she'd go for that—maybe I'm kind of old for it, but I never had the chance of college. I'd always thought architecture sounded kind of interesting, I thought maybe I could go to the university here and study that. I think she'd agree to it."

"Very commendable," said Jesse.

"Well, I don't feel right not doing a damn thing. I couldn't stop her buying me that car—well, she's used to having her own way. I was sorry she treated you like that the other day." He got up. "That's about all I wanted to say, Mr. Falkenstein. Thanks for listening. I just wanted you and Mrs. Garland to know how I feel."

"Thanks for coming in," said Jesse.

As the door closed he was thinking even harder about Mr. Smith. That was a very nice act, if it was an act, and what else would it be? And he wondered—that had all sounded so very plausible—if Charlene Garland had heard that, if she'd begin to change her mind about Mr. Smith. If she'd met him—the charmer in that boyish sense, whether it was naïve or studied— before she'd seen that letter, listened to her aunt's sentimentalities, would she have accepted him at face value, however reluctantly? At least, she might have reflected, he was cheering Aunt Ruth's old age.

That had been a very nice performance indeed. He wondered

LESLEY EGAN 55

if the various jobs Jerry Smith might have held had included any acting.

And the damned senseless verse kept running through his mind—"When will you pay me?/Say the bells of Old Bailey— When I grow rich,/Say the bells of Shoreditch."

He picked up Charlene Garland's letter again and then put it down and looked up the number. "Sorry to call you at work again," he said, when she came on the line. "Thanks very much for your letter."

"I hope it gave you some ideas."

"I already had some. I don't suppose you could tell me the names of any of the psychics your aunt once consulted?"

She said incredulously. "Twenty years ago? I wasn't even here. You do ask the queerest things, Mr. Falkenstein. Wait a minute. Oddly enough I do remember one of them. Mother mentioned it. I wouldn't have remembered, but you run across her name sometimes in the tabloids, she seems to be fairly well known now. Niland—Margaret Niland. Why on earth do you want to know that? These people are mostly fakes or hysterics, aren't they?"

"Not always. Thanks very much." He reflected sadly that it said something about the educational standards—and the materiality—of the twentieth century, that after a century of careful psychic research and all the mounds of evidence it had turned up, a reasonably intelligent woman could make that flat statement.

He got his hat and coat and said to the Gordons, "I'm taking off early. There's no hurry about that letter, it can go tomorrow."

It was threatening to rain again, and cold; they were into March now, and according to the old proverb it had come in with high winds. The rush-hour traffic hadn't got under way yet, but soon would. He went up Rossmoor to Santa Monica Boulevard, found a spot in a public lot, and walked back to an old six-story building in the middle of the block. There wasn't an elevator; he climbed to the third floor and walked halfway down the hall to a door on the left. The black painted legend on the upper frosted glass said, WESTERN ASSOCIATION FOR PSYCHIC RESEARCH.

He turned the knob and went in, to a narrow anteroom. It certainly wasn't an impressive set of offices, but rents anywhere were steep these days. He knew, of course, what the rent was; he was the Association's nominal treasurer.

Miss Duffy was adjusting a singularly unbecoming hat at the dingy mirror behind the receptionist's desk. "De Witt here?" asked Jesse.

"You just caught us, we'd have been gone in five minutes," said Miss Duffy serenely. William De Witt, lean and lank and dark, appeared in the doorway of his office.

"Well, Jesse, you don't often honor us these days. Do anything for you?"

"Depends," said Jesse. "Do you know Margaret Niland, William?"

De Witt regarded him with interest. "Most people in the field know of her. As it happens, I know her fairly well. We've both been mixed up with some experiments going on in the Psychology Department at UCLA, and we've shared the platform at a couple of seminars. Why?"

"I'd appreciate an introduction."

"Don't tell me you want to consult her? That's not so easy these days, she doesn't see just anybody. She's working almost exclusively with the law now, advising police looking for missing bodies and so on."

"That so? Gratifying that the boys in blue realize the sensitives can sometimes offer leads."

"And catch most of them admitting it, even when they use them. What do you want with Mrs. Niland?"

"She lives somewhere around here, doesn't she?"

"Pasadena. Apart from being a sensitive, she's a somewhat busy wife and mother, a damned good cook, and she makes a very mean martini."

"Be obliged," said Jesse, "if you'd provide me with an entrée to the presence. I want to ask her about a former client."

"My dear Jesse, she's frighteningly ethical."

"Oh, I think she'll be willing to talk to me when I explain it to her."

"Well, I'll give her a call when I get home. Sometime. I'll let you know. Unless she's off helping a sheriff somewhere to locate a downed plane—"

"Give me a call as soon as you know."

"I'll do that. And you can tell me all about it sometime when I'm not in a hurry. I'm supposed to have dinner with the president of the British SPR in an hour."

"Moving in exalted circles. Let me know, William."

"All right, all right."

4

Monday had passed and he hadn't got back to the FBI office; he might make time for that tomorrow. There was also the employment agency. He read to Davy before bed, and started some Bach on the stereo to aid cerebration. When he went upstairs at eleven o'clock Nell was sitting up in bed reading with Athelstane on the floor beside the bed and Murteza coiled in a tight circle on her lap. The wind was howling around the house. He prodded Athelstane awake and downstairs for a last run; Athelstane went reluctantly and didn't stay out long.

He had just switched out the bedside lamp when the phone rang, and he switched it on again and went across the bedroom to answer it; as he'd promised himself, there was a phone in every principal room in the house.

"I've just got hold of Margaret Niland," said De Witt. "She'll be pleased to see you tomorrow night at nine, if that's all right. I'll give you the address." It was a street in upper Pasadena.

"Thanks very much. I hope you told her I'm respectable and reasonably intelligent."

"At least she knows you're not a skeptic. I'd like to hear what it's all about sometime."

"When I have the time. Thanks, William."

Tuesday was a brilliantly sunny clear day, with the wind blowing a gale. Nell was bewailing all her bulbs. "I was so

pleased that they came up early—all the darling daffodils and
those special lilies—and they're getting blown to pieces! I like it
up here on the hill, away from the city, but there are drawbacks,
I'll bet it isn't nearly so bad farther down—"

"Drawbacks wherever you live," said Jesse absently.

"And when I think what I paid for all those bulbs—of course
the tulips and iris will be later, and I just hope this dies down—"

He checked at the office; he hadn't any appointments until the
afternoon. He drove down to Beverly Hills, to the hole-in-the-
wall office of the E. McGraw Employment Agency. He handed a
card to a plain-faced receptionist in a minute anteroom. "I'd like
to see Mrs. McGraw on a private matter, if she's got the time."

"I'll see, sir. It's Miss." She disappeared into an inner office,
came back and held the door for him. "You can come in, sir."

The inner office was a good deal larger, with file cabinets
around three sides, a bare-topped, scarred old desk holding only
a telephone, a desk pad, and a little wooden name sign that read
Elise McGraw. It seemed an unlikely first name for the woman
at the desk. She was a tall raw-boned woman with an angular
figure, a square plain face with strongly marked dark brows and
a firm mouth, pepper and salt hair cut crisply short, and her
dark eyes were direct and cool. She looked at his card. "How
can I help you, Mr. Falkenstein? You told Alice, a private matter."

He sat down in the chair beside the desk, without invitation.
He seemed to be telling Mrs. Traxler's story to everybody he
talked to, but it was the only way to get people to open up to
him. She listened impassively without any exclamations. "You
can see that one very likely source of the information would be
her servants. I'm after some information about them. I understand she usually hires them through you."

She nodded, and unbent to light a cigarette. "That's a cruel
thing to do to that woman," she said unexpectedly. "A vulnerable sort of woman—people with money can be vulnerable."

"Well, that's a word for it."

"Money's always a sort of shield, isn't it?"

"Did she hire many people through you? Servants stay with her very long?"

"I don't see any reason I shouldn't tell you," said Miss McGraw consideringly. "You could say I specialize in people with money. The kind who want efficient, dependable help, and can afford it. You might not think so, but there are a lot of wealthy people in this town who can afford the live-in permanent servants, and really good ones aren't that easy to find, you know. Not these days. Of course, there are all the show-business people, most of them"—she laughed—"more money than sense as they say. But there are a lot of others too. They want reliable people to run their houses for them and look after kids, all the domestic drudgery, and they'll pay for good service. If you ask me, it's one hell of a better deal for the right kind of people than the eight-to-five job, hassling with rush-hour traffic and high rents and difficult bosses. It's mostly pretty easy work, compared, and you get your living thrown in. Of course, not everybody wants to live in somebody else's house, but it can be a damned soft living, Mr. Falkenstein, when you think about it. You take Mrs. Traxler. She doesn't entertain much, what she wants is a woman to do the cooking, marketing, a little regular housework. She's considerate of her servants—mostly—and she's got a regular cleaning service to do all the basic heavy jobs, so the woman's only got to do a little dusting, cleaning—all the modern appliances in the kitchen, most of the bedrooms shut up and not being used, and it's the kind of work a woman would be doing in her own house anyway. She's particular, but she pays well and appreciates good service. Of course, all domestic jobs aren't quite that easy, but a lot are."

"What about the housekeeper she's got now? And I'd like to know if you can tell me anything about the servants with her back then—have you been in business that long, do you know anything about that?"

She said imperturbably, "I've been in this business thirty years, Mr. Falkenstein. Yes, I can tell you something about that. It's not nice to think that anybody I've placed with her would conspire to defraud the old lady, but people come all sorts, and

I can see it's one place for you to look. The woman with her now —let me look in the files." She went over to one of the file cases, labeled alphabetically, extracted a cardboard file, laid it on the desk and opened it. "Oh, yes. Ingrid Goodman, she's been with Mrs. Traxler nearly six years, she was new on my books when I got her the place. She seems to be quite satisfactory. She'd been working up north in San Francisco, she said she wanted to be in this area because she'd got family here. The woman who was with Mrs. Traxler before that"—she laughed shortly—"left for an unusual reason. She said there wasn't enough to do, no dinner parties or people coming in, she got bored. Just one old lady to look after. Well, she had been with Emil Kruger, that big producer, you know, and I suppose she enjoyed the glamour of all the socialites and big stars coming to dinner, and so on. She's with Carol Frawley now." He recognized the name: one of the latest TV lovelies. "You'd like to know something about the people who were with her when that awful kidnapping happened? I remember pretty well because of that, but let's see what I've got down." She leafed through the file. "I keep pretty complete records. There was a couple, man and wife, Albert and Thelma Dillon, housekeeper and chauffeur. They'd been with an old lady in San Marino until she died. At the time they'd been with the Traxlers for nearly ten years. Then there was a full-time maid, what was her name, oh, Rose Shaw. It was her first job with me, she was only about twenty. The nursemaid, Katherine Drake, was English—she was something of a character," and Miss McGraw smiled. "She'd come to this country with an English family attached to the Embassy here, and left them when the children got too old for a nurse. I'd placed her for a while with, let's see, oh, yes, that director, John Gleason—you may remember, he was killed in a plane crash—and his wife went back East and Miss Drake wanted to stay in California. That was when she went to Mrs. Traxler. It was nearly twenty-six years ago, by this. The Traxler boy would have been just a baby, I suppose."

"Those were all the live-in servants?" asked Jesse.

"Yes." And she added baldly, "They were all let go right after the kidnapping."

Startled, Jesse said, "You don't say. Why?"

"It's the reason I remembered it all so clearly." She sat back and lit another cigarette. "It was all damnably unfair. Of course, they'd all been investigated by the FBI, that was only to be expected. I even had a couple of G-men come nosing around here asking me what I knew about them. But they were all exonerated. I suppose you know there was never any charge brought on anybody, the authorities were satisfied that none of the servants had anything to do with the kidnapping. But Mrs. Traxler was apparently in such a hysterical state that she suspected everybody and anybody and just didn't want any of them around. She fired them all just a few days later, and she even refused to give them references—not," said Miss McGraw reminiscently, "that that made much difference."

"You don't tell me," said Jesse. "Why not?"

"Mr. Traxler came to see me and apologized about it, he was really very nice, and he said he'd write them all references himself. But it was a—well, a funny position. It wasn't easy to find new jobs for any of them." Miss McGraw's smooth broad brow wrinkled.

"You mean because—"

She nodded. "That was it. People were chary of having somebody in the house who'd been mixed up with a crime. A thing like that. It was a kidnapping, you see. None of them had had anything to do with that—we've got to realize that, because the authorities never charged anybody. There wasn't any evidence, but—people don't think straight when it comes to a thing like that." She drew strongly on the cigarette, emitted a cloud of smoke and after a moment of silence said, "Well, you take Katherine Drake. A perfectly nice woman, very efficient and experienced. I had two openings for a children's nurse on the books at the time, with families right here in town, and both women turned her down when they heard she'd been with the Traxlers. It was just after the stories about the kidnapping had been in the papers, you see. I pointed out that she had a per-

fectly good reference from Mr. Traxler, and they both said the
same thing, but not Mrs. Traxler, and why had she been let go?
There must have been something—I said the authorities knew
the servants were completely innocent, but they wouldn't have
her at any price. Not with their children, thank you. Of course it
was irrational, but you can see how their minds worked. I
couldn't get her a place as a nurse, and she was furious about it
—that was all she wanted—she seemed to have a funny snob-
bish idea that that was a long step up from being any kind of
domestic servant. She was a children's nanny and nothing else. I
finally persuaded her to take a job as companion-housekeeper to
an old lady in West Hollywood, but she didn't like it. She kept
pestering me to find her a place as a nurse."

"Do you know where she is now?"

"Sure," said Miss McGraw with a crooked smile. "The old lady
died, and I did get her a job as a children's nurse, with that
actor, Clive Adams—that was six or seven years later when people had forgotten about the kidnapping—and she didn't like it at
all. Complained that the children were brats and the family just
riffraff—he'd been divorced a few times, and it was one of those
households with your kids and my kids and our kids, you know?
I found her a couple of other jobs, but it was the same thing. As
it happened, they were all with show-business people, that is
Hollywood show-business people, and she's a hell of a snob—she
looks down her nose at these upstarts."

"Where is she now?" asked Jesse patiently.

"Oh, she's in a lovely spot now, she has been for the last ten
years. She claims she doesn't like it, but she knows when she's
got it made." Miss McGraw laughed. "She's with Beatrice Ogilvie—you know the English actress—she's retired from films now
except for an occasional cameo part, but of course she's loaded.
Scatterbrained sort of female, but there's something quite nice
and kind about her for all that. And she's a private sort of
woman, doesn't like a raft of servants around, and Miss Drake is
just right for her—they suit each other to a T. Drake supervises
the people who come to clean the apartment, and if I know her
she bosses them around like a sergeant major, and treats Miss

Ogilvie like a nursery charge—she's a good cook, by the way—
and they both love it."

"Here?" said Jesse.

"Right here. Loma Linda Drive right in town. I really don't
know that I can see Katherine Drake conspiring with anybody
to defraud Mrs. Traxler."

"What about the rest of them?"

"Well, the Dillons went back East. I couldn't find them anything, either together or separately, people turned them down for
the same reason, and they'd come here from some little town in
Pennsylvania, they decided to go back there. I think he had a
brother with some kind of business where he could get a job.
The maid, I don't know anything about her. I got her another
job but she didn't stay in it long, got fired for incompetence, and
I didn't keep her on my books. Oh, I could give you her home
address then, but that's a long time back."

"What about the servants since?"

"Well"—she was leafing through the folder—"after the Dillons
Mrs. Traxler had a housekeeper named Sarah Newby, she was
with her about seven years and then she left—she was getting
on for seventy, and she retired and went to live with a married
daughter, I seem to remember it was Arizona somewhere." Jesse
sighed. "Then she had another rather elderly woman, Frances
Johnson, she was only with her a couple of years before she had
a heart attack and had to quit work—she died right after that.
Then she had the woman who got bored because there wasn't
enough to do, her name was Susan Allway."

"And where is she now, you know?"

"Sure, she's with the Jay Petersons. He's a director and they're
very social, a lot of coming and going and parties. I expect Mrs.
Allway's enjoying herself, anyway she's been with them for
seven years and hasn't come in to ask me to find her another job.
And since then Mrs. Traxler has had the Goodman woman."

"What about the handyman-chauffeur?"

"Well, she had the same one for years after the Dillons—a
man named Metcalf, he was a quiet sort who suited her, but
when he was getting on in age he left and went to live with

some relative up north, I couldn't say where. That was a couple of years ago." Jesse sighed again. "Then I found her a man named Wilson, very briefly, and he turned out to be a drunk. It was the first job I'd found for him, and naturally I don't have him on my books now. The man with her now is Howard Hoffman, and I hope," said Miss McGraw cynically, "he appreciates the job. Driving an old lady around shopping and calling on friends about three times a week, looking after the car, doing a few odd jobs in the house, and he gets his pay and meals and a nice little apartment over the garage. But it's her money."

"Well, thanks very much," said Jesse. "Could I have Miss Drake's address? And the woman who got bored? And is that all you know about Mrs. Goodman?"

She glanced again at the sheet before her. "Well, she's a widow."

"Thanks. All that doesn't say a great deal, but thanks."

"I hope you can find out something and rescue the poor soul from the con man," said Miss McGraw. "That's a cruel thing to do to her."

"Debatable point," said Jesse wryly. "She's enjoying it."

He went back to the car and drove back to Hollywood, to the FBI office. He talked to the same man, Upjohn, at the front desk, who went away and presently came back to say, "Mr. Bradshaw can give you a few minutes, sir. If you'd come this way."

They were all alike, the Feds. He saw Bradshaw in a little cubbyhole of an office in a row of cubbyholes at the rear of the larger outer office. Bradshaw was about fifty, bland, well tailored, polite, noncommittal. He gave Jesse the only other chair and listened to what he had to say courteously. At the conclusion of the story he passed a hand over his bald spot and said, "That's a new caper on me, Mr. Falkenstein. Of course, it's a set of rather specialized circumstances, isn't it? And the woman's obviously damned gullible."

"You can see, if I could get hold of anything to prove he couldn't possibly be her son—"

"Yes, of course. It's all a little offbeat. I'm not familiar with the case—it'd be before I was transferred out here by what you say. There might be something in the inactive file. You do realize that it's against our policy to discuss cases with civilians, but since this is evidently off our books—let me see what I can turn up." He was away for quite a while, finally came back and said, "I didn't realize it was quite that far back. Anything on it still in our dead files would be on microfilm either at the office downtown or back in Washington. All I can tell you, Mr. Falkenstein, is that none of the agents presently attached to this office or anywhere in the area were here that long ago. But there's one man you might contact, who might be able to tell you something. Kendall, Brian Kendall. He retired just last year and is still in the area—Upjohn reminded me just now. I can give you his address, I looked it up for you." He passed over a sheet torn from a memo pad. "He'd been in this office for nearly thirty years."

"Thanks so much," said Jesse. "Would that microfilm be available to me if it is in your office downtown?"

"You might have to go through a few channels," said Bradshaw impassively.

Jesse went back to the Mercedes in the public lot. The address was in Encino. He had appointments in the afternoon, but at this hour the freeways would be relatively empty. He got on the right one and once he got off it in Encino he asked directions at a Shell station; he didn't know this town.

It was a broad quiet residential street, lined with newish houses surrounded by lawns and trees. The one he wanted was on a corner. He pushed the bell four times before he gave up and started back to the car. As he stepped off the porch a man came down the driveway of the next house and glanced at Jesse, hesitated, and said, "You want the Kendalls? They're not home —they're up in Bakersfield visiting family. I think they'll be home tomorrow or next day."

Jesse thanked him. He swore at himself for not calling first, but you rather expected a man retired to be at home, pottering about the garden or watching TV. And he really didn't know where all this was getting him. It was all a handful of nothing.

He started back for Hollywood feeling discouraged, but at the same time doing some thinking about those servants.

* * *

At nine o'clock he looked at Margaret Niland in her pleasant, slightly shabby living room and liked what he saw. She had, of course, a very high reputation as a psychic, in circles that knew about psychic research. She might be fifty or a bit more, a little plump, with graying brown hair in a neat knob on top of her head; she had a round rather pretty face and bright brown eyes; she was very conventionally, and rather dowdily, dressed in a brown skirt and beige blouse, with no jewelry but a wedding ring. She looked like a very ordinary woman, a woman you might meet in the dentist's waiting room or pushing a cart at the supermarket, but the psychic gift was more frequently visited on the ordinary person than on the exotic.

She surveyed him interestedly and said, "Mr. De Witt said you're trustworthy, Mr. Falkenstein, whatever he meant by that," and the brown eyes twinkled at him. "If it's something to do with my work, we may as well go down to my study—my husband's at a club meeting, but he'll be back at any time, and if it's something private—"

"You might say it is," said Jesse. She took him down the hall to a square room furnished as a study, with two walls of bookshelves, a small desk, Danish modern furniture. They sat down and she refused a cigarette but pushed an ashtray toward him.

"What did you want to see me about?"

He went through the tale again. "I gather that for some time after the kidnapping Mrs. Traxler started consulting every psychic she heard about, but the only one I know she definitely visited is you. And it's a long while back. You probably wouldn't remember—you'll have seen a lot of people since. I think it'd be at least eighteen or nineteen years ago."

She was looking concerned. "As Mr. De Witt probably told you—and he said you'll be familiar with how we work, you're not the average skeptical layman—ordinarily I wouldn't discuss a client's business. But this is a little different, I can see. To hoax that poor woman—well, what exactly are you after?"

"Damn it," he said, "I don't suppose you'd remember a thing you saw for her. I don't even know how many times you saw her."

She smiled at him almost mischievously. "It always surprises people—the kind of people who expect a psychic to be draped in Gypsy scarves and all that jazz—to find that I keep very complete files. Yes, I see a lot of people—I've been a practicing psychic for over thirty years—and of course it would be impossible for me to remember exactly what I said to everybody. But like most of us, I like to check up on myself, you see. On my batting average. And the SPR, and a good many other organizations doing research, like to keep a check on me too. To see how good or bad I am."

"You're supposed to be pretty good."

Her smile was a little rueful. "Not anything to boast about, just something you're born with or not, and you have to work at it, you know—you can't just wait for it to come, you have to practice and work at it. You probably know that I haven't been a consulting psychic for a long time now, in the sense that I give readings to anybody who asks—I've never charged any clients, of course—for the last fifteen years I've been working exclusively with research groups. About the only clients I accept now are police officers asking for help."

"So William said. It's interesting to know some of them come asking."

She laughed a little wryly. "And some of them are the absolute skeptics, but they come to me because they know I've been of help to other police forces. But it's only about one out of a hundred who does any talking about it or offers thanks in public."

"I believe you."

"But your Mrs. Traxler—" She got up and went over to the bookshelves across the room. "That long ago, I was hosting a daytime radio program on psychic research, and I was still giving readings to the public by appointment. That got to be just too exhausting, I had to give it up. But I've always kept very full notes on every reading I've ever done. A long time ago I was advised to do that by the people at the SPR." She came back with two thick loose-leaf notebooks, and he saw that nearly four shelves of that bookcase held others. "Maybe some day I'll write my autobiography. Let's see if I can find the name—these ought to be the right years." She leafed through slowly, put one book aside, tried the other. "Well, if you're sure I saw the woman it's got to be somewhere." She took the notebooks back, got another. Sitting beside him she leafed through it patiently. The sheets were covered, he saw, with fine clear handwriting. He sat back and waited.

Presently she said, "You were out by a year, Mr. Falkenstein. It was seventeen years ago. Mrs. Traxler." He saw that it was a fairly long entry; he could see over her shoulder that the writing was full of abbreviations and contractions, an aid to memory rather than precise prose. "Oh, yes, this reminds me very well. Like a lot of others she'd heard the radio program, that was why she came. Yes, she wanted to know about her boy, if he was alive or dead. Yes—she was a sentimental, not very intelligent woman, but I was sorry for her, by what I've got down here. I remember it very well now, because of the kidnapping. That was terrible."

"And what did you see for her—tell her?"

"Yes, it isn't always the same thing, I see you know that. You have to judge the people, there are some who can take bad news and live with it, and others who can't. If you see death for the one you're reading for, well, that's a thing you just don't tell, except in very rare circumstances. But in this case, I felt it would be—unkind—to raise any false hopes." She was scanning the lines of writing slowly. "I had to tell her her boy was dead," she said soberly. "I could see him quite clearly, and I saw him dead—a little blond boy in blue pajamas—and he was in a car, a sedan I think, it was at night, and there were either two or three other people in the car. He was lying across someone's lap, I couldn't tell if it was a man or a woman, but I'm pretty sure one of them was a woman—and I saw quite clearly that he was dead. He wasn't breathing. And the car was on a mountain road—at least it was a curving steep road."

"Oh," said Jesse. "That's interesting." He thought of the narrow, curving, steep streets in the Mt. Olympus Estates. "You didn't see how he died?"

"Just, he wasn't breathing. I had the definite impression that the people in the car were arguing about something. That's about it. But what else I put down here—" She laughed a little bitterly. "The woman told me I was lying to her, that I was a big fake because a lot of other sensitives had told her he was alive. She mentioned a lot of names I didn't know, and then she said that Helen Fiedler had told her he was alive, and everybody knew she was the greatest medium there was, she'd told her that he was alive when she went to one of her seances, and she had a private consultation too—Helen Fiedler had said she'd have news of him within a year. My God."

"I don't recognize the name," said Jesse.

"No, you'd be too young. She got a lot of publicity about thirty years ago, some of the movie crowd took her up. She used to hold old-fashioned seances with a trumpet, if you'll believe me, and claimed to produce materializations. She charged some fancy prices."

"Good God," said Jesse. "Not that some valid evidence didn't come that way, but of all the invitations to trickery—"

"A couple of local SPR members detected her in fraud the first time they had a look at her, but of course all her faithful fans didn't believe a word of it, they were just jealous because she was better than their favorite mediums—"

"Broken record. Yes, evidently Mrs. Traxler was what you'd call catholic in her tastes, and of course completely ignorant, no judgment at all. She probably went to everybody and anybody. Gifted psychic will answer three questions for five dollars, include birth date—down to Madam Natasha in a booth at the Venice pier, a dollar for ten minutes of garbled palmistry."

"People will be such idiots, I know," she said tiredly. "It makes you wonder. If any psychics really knew all there was to know about everything, we'd all be millionaires playing the races or the stock market."

"Well, you told me what I wanted to know, thanks."

"I don't see how it helps you at all, Mr. Falkenstein. And I can be wrong. Every psychic can be wrong. We're not infallible. And anyway, she didn't believe me then, so she's not going to believe it all these years later."

"But I might," said Jesse. "You're a check, do you see? You could put it like that. A check on the few facts we've got. You aren't often wrong on a thing like that, are you? You definitely saw the boy dead?"

She said ruefully, "Don't take it as gospel truth. I can be wrong about anything. I've been wrong a lot of times—it, whatever it is, doesn't always operate at the same level of efficiency—it comes and goes, and it can be frustrating. But looking over my notes, I do feel the boy was dead, yes. But it's possible that I was influenced by the fact that I knew it had been a kidnapping —she'd told me that. Because that's what you expect in a kidnapping, isn't it?"

"That's true," agreed Jesse cautiously. "But I'm glad to have heard this, Mrs. Niland, and thanks for the cooperation."

"I just hope you can do something about that poor woman."

"So do I, but I'm beginning to be sorry her niece picked me to consult."

* * *

On Wednesday morning he called Garrett to pass on those additional names of the former servants. Garrett said, "Now really, Falkenstein. Any commission within reason we'll undertake, but you don't really expect me to locate somebody named Metcalf somewhere up north? Or the woman said to have moved to Arizona?"

"Never said so."

"Or these Dillons somewhere in Pennsylvania?"

"No. Think the caper originated here. But Miss McGraw's revelation about that summary firing of the staff could set us thinking a little harder about those people. Especially the nursemaid, if you follow me. Of course, the Traxler woman was demented about the boy, not thinking straight, but an unjust act like that could have triggered the hell of a grudge."

"Oh, I see it, I see it."

"I don't suppose the maid is worth any consideration—"

"I'll agree with you. When all you've got is an address twenty-one years old. In a city of seven million. I'm happy you don't expect us to locate her for you."

"She sounds as if she was a fairly unreliable type, but not to the extent of conspiring to defraud."

"At least not twenty-one years later."

"I suppose it's too early to ask if you've turned up anything."

"Nothing of much interest. Your fair-haired boy is keeping his nose very, very clean. Allen says he must be damn bored. Even if he was brought up a Methodist, there is a limit, and a young fellow likes a little fun now and then. The car she bought him, by the way, is that new Chrysler sports model."

"You don't say. She laid out a piece of change for that."

"You lay out a piece of change for any car these days. He seems to stick fairly close to that house, and I'll agree with Allen that he's probably feeling bored. Still ingratiating himself with the old woman—"

"Or not antagonizing her. Too strong a word. Worrying her. In any way," said Jesse. "She's not used to having her darling Tommy back with her yet. And she'd say, and think she meant it, that she wants him to have friends of his own, go and play—maybe the country club where he'd meet a nice class of people and wouldn't it show that he was taking after his dear father—"

"What are you talking about?"

"—but if he really showed any signs of doing that, or, God forbid, acquired a pretty girl friend, she'd be jealous as hell, and that he knows. What has he been doing? Did they go to church on Sunday?"

"Nope. Neither of them. He's hit a bar on Fairfax a couple of times—quiet respectable place. One or two scotch and sodas is all. Hasn't talked to anybody but the bartender. He went to a movie yesterday afternoon."

"Porn house?"

"What, a well brought up Methodist boy? Of course not. A place down on Western runs the oldies. It was a nineteen-fifty musical."

"Anything else?"

"He's driven around some, looking sort of aimless. Down to the beach and back."

"Keeping his nose clean. Discouraging."

"What the hell did you expect?" asked Garrett. "The caper's all set up and operating. He's got no need to have secret meetings with a co-conspirator. Allen pointed that out."

"Yes. So says Solomon, *The thoughts of mortal men are miserable, and our devices are but uncertain.* You just carry on for a while."

And instead of getting on with the paper work on the damage suit he slid down in his chair and thought about that possible grudge, rankling. A long while back, but it was the kind of thing to foster a grudge. The Dillons seemed to be out of it, back East, and he thought this deal had been set up right here. But you couldn't exclude anybody; anybody who'd ever been in that house, listened to Mrs. Traxler's reminiscences, had known enough to be the source. The fact that Jerry Smith had grown up in California didn't say that he'd stayed here; he could have run into any of those people anywhere. But of all of them, Jesse liked the nursemaid for the part better than the others. She was the one who had been the most victimized by that firing, that very summary firing. Granted, in the absence of the boy, she'd have been out of a job anyway, but she'd been fired at once, along with the rest, before anybody could be sure the boy wouldn't be returned, and despite the fact that the Feds had exonerated the servants; that was what had been in those prospective employers' minds—the Traxlers must have had some reason, would be the little niggling whisper. Oh, yes. And the nursemaid —"a character"—had been for some while at least deprived of her regular line of work, and tainted with greater suspicion than the others, simply because she was the nursemaid. Nursemaid to the little boy lost, stolen and vanished in the night, and nobody would take the chance—irrational as it was, not until memories had faded—and she could well have harbored a king-sized grudge on Mrs. Traxler, might still be harboring one. He thought he'd like to have a look at the nursemaid for himself.

But he had other things to think about than Mrs. Traxler and Jerry Smith. There would be a rather complicated divorce settlement to arrange for one of the new clients, there was that damage suit, a couple of other divorces: as usual, there was business on hand. Leave it for the moment and see what the private eyes might turn up. He felt exasperated with the whole sorry business, and started to make notes about the divorce settlement with some relief at getting back to rationalities.

* * *

Clock had got used to James Gilchrist tagging after him in the last few days, but he didn't blame Gilchrist for abandoning the Hollywood Division today. They were hard at the legwork on that damned double homicide, and of course it would all come to nothing in the end—it was just going through the motions. That porn movie house had some regular patrons, known to the ticket seller and usher, and they had turned up a handful of them. So far, nobody had admitted sitting anywhere near the Taylor girl and Lopez; nobody ever would. More useful information had been turned up from prodding at Wilma's girl friends, for the names of men she'd dated; they had four names now and Petrovsky and Mantella were out hunting for those men while Clock finished typing the latest report.

He had just ripped the triplicate forms out of the typewriter when Gilchrist came in. "Well, I thought you were downtown gathering stories from the lab men at SID."

"I was," said Gilchrist morosely, "and I collected a couple of good cases for the book, but they're all so busy they haven't much time for me. I'm still doing a little burn about the Traxler thing, damn it, it's a teaser. I just dropped in to have lunch with you, thought I'd locate Falkenstein's office and see what he's turned up on it, if anything."

The phone rang on Clock's desk and he picked it up. "Holly-

wood Division LAPD, Sergeant Clock." He listened, said, "Oh.
Well, thanks very much," and scribbled some notes. "Spell that.
Right. Okay, we'll be on it." He put the phone down. "That's a
long step on. That was our lab. We've just identified the
redhead, they got the kickback from the Feds on her prints. She
worked for the Post Office at that town in Nevada, Henderson.
Her name was Sally Fisher."

"Congratulations," said Gilchrist.

"And Jesse's usually busy, but he does go out for lunch. I can
call Nevada later—I'll give him a ring and we can meet him
somewhere."

Over lunch at a restaurant on Wilshire, they heard about Miss
McGraw's revelations and were interested. Gilchrist said, "If
anybody was holding a grudge, the likeliest possibility is that
nursemaid all right."

"And people will hold the grudges," said Jesse.

"Bea Ogilvie," said Clock reflectively. "I always liked her—
she's no spring chicken these days, but a hell of a lot more talent
than most of these beauty-contest winners they try to put over as
instant stars. Funny that nursemaid should end up with her. I
saw somewhere lately, she's in a Broadway play that just
opened. But that psychic—well for God's sake, Jesse, I know you
put some stock in that kind of thing, but what could it mean?
It's nothing to give any lead."

"It could say quite a lot," said Jesse mildly. "No leads, no. If I
can ever get hold of that Fed—"

"So maybe," said Gilchrist, "she's holding down the fort alone.
Unless she's off on vacation."

"Who?" asked Clock.

"The nanny," said Gilchrist impatiently, "if the Ogilvie
woman's in New York. Your private eyes are just taking a look
from the distance, Falkenstein. What do you say we call on her
if she's there, see what reaction we get?"

"Damn it, I've got paper work to do. I haven't an appointment
until three o'clock, but—"

"Come on," said Gilchrist briskly. "The paper work will wait
for you."

"And I suppose I'd better get back to the office and talk to Nevada," said Clock. "Try to find out what the redhead was doing over here. But I'll be interested to hear what you might get, Jesse." He was bored with the current jobs at the office. It would be good to get home to Fran and the baby.

5

The apartment building on Loma Linda Drive wasn't new but quietly elegant, red brick and stucco; it probably contained no more than eight or ten units. There was a large swimming pool at one side of it, and manicured landscaping. Ogilvie was listed on the second floor, by the mail boxes, in Apartment F. They climbed carpeted stairs and found the door, and Jesse pushed the bell. After a moment the door opened halfway. A suspicious voice said, "Miss Ogilvie's not at home."

"Miss Drake?" said Jesse. "I think it's you we want to see." He handed over a card.

She looked at it doubtfully. "I don't know any lawyers. What do you want?"

"We'd just like to ask you a few questions, that's all. May we come in?"

"What's it all about?"

She looked much as he had imagined her, a short stout woman; she wore a printed cotton housedress with a white bib apron over it. But he hadn't heard about the shiny raven-black hair in a tight knob on her neck, the apple-red cheeks, the little snapping black eyes.

She gave way reluctantly. "Miss Ogilvie's away, but I s'pose she wouldn't mind—what's this all about? What does a lawyer want with me?"

It was a very elegant living room, with period French furniture, an oriental carpet, what might be a couple of original Impressionist paintings on two walls.

Jesse had debated about an approach, and said bluntly, "I think you once worked for Mrs. Thomas Traxler, didn't you?"

Her expression hardened. "That was a long time ago."

"Yes, at the time of the kidnapping—when their son was kidnapped. You were his nurse, weren't you?"

"I was, and that was a wicked, wicked thing, that poor darling stolen away. I never got over that. I'd had him from the month, he was like my own. Some wicked man taking him away and murdering him, and Mr. Traxler paid the money, but they never got Tommy back. I never got over it. But that's a long time ago, why should you come around asking about it now?" She perched stiffly on one end of the long couch, and in lieu of invitation Jesse and Gilchrist took the chairs opposite.

Jesse said, "Well, Mrs. Traxler thinks he's come back now."

"Tommy?" she asked sharply.

"Somebody pretending to be Tommy. Everybody was sure he was dead, weren't they? But Mrs. Traxler never believed it, went on hoping he was alive—somewhere."

She said a little grimly, "She might do that." Her English accent was softened by years in this country, but there was still more than a trace of it in her speech. "What do you mean?"

"A young man pretending to be Tommy, and he seems to know a lot about Tommy and that household, enough to convince Mrs. Traxler that he's really her son."

"Well, fancy that," she said slowly. "After all these years. But it couldn't be because Tommy's dead. Mr. Traxler came and told me, he said that those government policemen were sure he was dead, those wicked people had killed him, that was a while after."

"Yes," said Jesse, "and this fellow's getting money from Mrs. Traxler. We'd like to prove he couldn't be Tommy and stop that."

She said with unexpected shrewdness, "I expect that will be Mr. Traxler's niece, Miss Charlene, she's a nice young lady. I

saw in the paper when Mr. Traxler died, and I expect most of
the money'd go to Miss Charlene when Mrs. Traxler goes. They
always said she had a bad heart, but she'll be way up in the sixties now—so she's still alive—well, I never. That's a downright
wicked thing too, trick her that way. Mr. Traxler said they were
sure Tommy was dead."

"But you haven't much reason to feel sympathetic for her,
have you? After the way she fired you without notice when that
happened."

She fired up on the instant. "Sympathetic? I hope I'd feel decent sympathy for any woman who'd lost her only child in such
a wicked way, but you're right, sir, she hadn't any call to treat
me or the others like she did, we all felt it something terrible,
and I felt it worse, I was struck all of a heap, it grieved me sore.
I'd been pleased to get that position with Mrs. Traxler, a real
English lady, and it was a nice household, I always got on with
her fine, she trusted Tommy to me every way, like a lady would.
Nearly six years I was like one of the family, and Tommy like
my own—he was a dear little boy and between us we were
bringing him up the right way. Oh, she had some old-fashioned
notions, but sometimes that's the best kind. And the staff was
treated real proper, it was a nice house to be in. Everybody was
that fond of Tommy, that Mrs. Dillon fixing favorite things for
him, he was just crazy for her orange meringues—" Jesse
thought suddenly that Charlene Garland had forgotten the orange meringues in her letter; she had mentioned it when she first
talked to him. "And Dillon letting him pretend to drive the car
and all. That Rose girl was a flighty sort, but good hearted
enough. We were all just struck to the heart when it happened,
that wicked cruel thing, he was like my own, I'd had him from
the month, I was just as sore grieved as his mother and father,
all of us were—and to be treated like that—told to get out without a moment's notice as if we were a pack of criminals! That
had been my home for over five years, Tommy as much my own
as hers. I'd had all the care of him since he was born, and he
loved me as much as I loved him. Judy he called me, by way of
my telling him stories about the Punch and Judy shows on the

seafront at home—and he liked to hear about my old home in England. If she'd acted as I expected, like any woman would, we'd've shared all the grief, she knew I loved Tommy, she must have known—but to treat me like that!"

"Yes, it wasn't very fair, was it?"

"It was not, sir, and it was a terrible grief to me. Mr. Traxler, he tried to be kind, he came to see me and said she was nearly off her head with sorrowing about Tommy and didn't rightly know what she was doing—poor man, it was a terrible thing for him too, his only child and he wasn't a young man—oh, dear, that was an awful time. And just because I'd been Tommy's nurse, nobody would have me for their children, as if I'd had anything to do with that terrible thing—I can't say I didn't feel it something cruel."

"Yes," said Gilchrist. "If you felt you had a reason to have a grudge on Mrs. Traxler, it was only natural."

She had been gazing at the floor as memories poured out; she looked up at him. "Of course I was angry at the woman, why wouldn't I be? It was hard on me, but what I felt the worst, I'd thought she knew how I loved Tommy, as much as she did or his father, and her treating me like that, as if I hadn't been there above a day, didn't think of the place as my home—" She looked at Jesse. "But you're telling me, there's someone pretending to be Tommy now? That's queer—it couldn't be, they were nearly sure he was dead. Killed by those wicked people. Mr. Traxler came and told me, that was afterward, I was still out of work, but he knew I'd want to know. It was nice of him. They'd found a body, and those government police thought it was Tommy."

"This young fellow seems to know all about Tommy, and that household. He says he remembers you too, Miss Drake. And his toys, and little pieces he used to recite to visitors."

"Well, I never," she said. "Yes, that was one of her old-fashioned notions, to get him to say pieces for people when they called, or came to tea. I taught him a lot of little rhymes to say out of the nursery book. She'd have him downstairs when people came to tea—but how would this fellow know that?"

"Somebody," said Gilchrist, "who knew that could have told

him—one of the staff there then—somebody who's worked for
Mrs. Traxler since, she talks about Tommy a lot and the kidnapping a good deal."

"But who'd want to do that?"

"When she's convinced that Tommy's come back to her, she's
handing over quite a little money to him, Miss Drake."

"Oh," she said slowly, "I suppose she would do that. You
could see she was spoiling him. I used to be a little strict with
him, you can't let a child get the notion the whole world's revolving around him. But she was old when he was born, probably never thought to have a child of her own, it was natural.
Yes, I see. She wouldn't forget it, she'd be remembering it all the
time. Goodness knows I never forgot it. But I don't know who
could have helped the man like that, sir. I don't know anything
about the people that worked for the Traxlers after that. I've
never laid eyes on Mrs. Traxler from that day to this. It—it
couldn't really be Tommy, could it? Mr. Traxler said they were
nearly sure, but nearly isn't quite—do you think he could really
be Tommy? Even if the kidnappers didn't bring him back—if he
wasn't killed—and grew up somehow—and remembered who he
was?" She looked suddenly both doubtful and eager.

"It doesn't seem very likely, does it?" said Jesse. "Was he a
bright little boy, Miss Drake? Knew his own name and where he
lived?"

"Oh, yes, sir!" she said, with remembered pride. "He was a
clever child, he learned all the little verses real quick and easy,
he was a little shy with people he didn't know, but he was
bright—he knew his own address, not that there was any chance
of his getting lost away from home, but he'd just started going
to the nursery school, it was a little private school in Beverly
Hills, he'd been going there that summer and he liked it fine.
Dillon drove him every morning and brought him home at noon.
He was going to start going to Sunday school the very week it
happened, he knew some little prayers to say already, I'd told
him some stories about Jesus—oh, he was such a dear little boy—"

"The kidnappers wouldn't have kept him, you know," said
Jesse. "Nobody but Mrs. Traxler thinks this is really Tommy."

"I'd know!" she said vigorously. "You let me take a look at that man, I could tell you if it's really Tommy. I'd know for sure."

"I don't suppose you would, Miss Drake. Twenty-one years—"

"Oh, I'd know! I had all the care of him day and night, and any woman'd know what I mean—there's a feel about a child you've had all the care of, you'd recognize him years later, oh, maybe not all by looks because children change but—I can't explain it—by the feel of the person he'd be. I'd know."

Gilchrist said, "Mrs. Traxler thinks she knows."

She snorted in a ladylike way. "Her—it's not the same—she's his mother but she'd never bathed him, dressed him, been with him most of every day since he was born! Oh, she loved him— maybe too much, if you can love a child too much—she'd have him down with her afternoons whether there were callers or not, and hear him recite, and hold him on her lap and play with him, but maybe for a couple of hours, and then he'd come back to me in the nursery. And his father loved him too, but he was at business all day and he'd only see Tommy an hour or two in the evening. You let me take a look at this man and I'll tell you if it's Tommy or not."

"Yes, I can see what you mean," said Jesse. "But it isn't likely. Why would the kidnappers keep him? Or just not bring him back?"

She said doubtfully, without conviction, "He was such a darling little boy—I don't know. Oh, dear, you've brought it all back to me, sir—talking about it—all those years ago, but I remember it all so clear! It was just after Miss Charlene got married, the wedding reception was at the house, there were caterers in and all such lovely decorations, and Tommy had a new little blue suit, Mrs. Traxler had wanted him to be in the wedding and carry the ring, but Mr. Traxler said he was too little— but they had him down to the reception—I remember I had to go down and fetch him, it had got to be way past his bedtime— and everybody was making a fuss of him, he looked so darling in that little suit. I remember telling him not to get any notions in his head he was better than any other little boy. But he was a good child for all that, I don't think she'd've been able to spoil

him much as he grew up spite of everything. Oh, dear, that was
a night, there must have been a hundred people there, and Miss
Charlene so pretty in her wedding dress, and her young man so
handsome—to think what was just ahead—" She fumbled for a
handkerchief and wiped her eyes. "It wasn't more than two
weeks later, you know. That had been such a hot day—that was
a hot summer—and I don't mind it in the ordinary way, but it
had got just too hot—I wouldn't let Tommy play in the back
yard that afternoon, I was afraid the sun would be too much for
him. I kept him in, but it was nearly that hot in the house, so
close and stuffy like. You see, the air conditioning wasn't on. The
man had come just the day before and said the motor was burned
out, they'd need to put in a new one, and Mr. Traxler had got
some electric fans to use until it was fixed. That one big police-
man saying I wouldn't have heard anything in Tommy's room
because the fan was running! I'd've heard him in an instant if
he'd waked and called me—when you're used to looking after a
child you sleep light, any little call'd wake you—and sometimes
he had nightmares. I'd've heard Tommy call—but it must have
been, they stopped him making any noise at all. The bathroom
door was closed into his room—it wasn't latched—but of course
I had my light on after he went to sleep and any little smidgen
of light bothered him—he never was like some children who
have to have a night light. And by the time I turned out my
light it hadn't cooled off hardly at all, so of course I kept the fan
on, it was by the window. And my alarm went off at the usual
time and I got up and got dressed and went to get Tommy up—
and there was his little bed empty and the covers all thrown
back and he wasn't there—I never had such a fright in my life,
my heart just seemed to stop—and I ran quick down to the
Traxlers' room to see if he'd gone there, only he never did, and
Mr. Traxler said maybe he'd waked early and got out of the
house to play in the back yard. Only all the doors were still
locked—so he called the police—but before they came we looked
at Tommy's room again, and saw that the window screen was cut
right out, and that ladder there—and that was when we knew it
was a kidnapping. How those wicked, wicked people do. Mrs.

Traxler fainted dead away, and I couldn't stop crying, it was Mrs. Dillon had to run to get some ammonia for her—and then the police came—" She was sniffing into the handkerchief. "Oh, you bring it all back. It was a terrible time. We were all just crazy with worry. And then just three days later, with all those police coming and going and not knowing if Tommy was alive or dead, Mrs. Traxler tells us we'll have to go. That minute, she doesn't want us in the house. You can see how we felt it, and I felt it worse than the others."

"Very understandable," agreed Jesse. "But you wouldn't have any idea who might have wanted to trick Mrs. Traxler to think Tommy has come back?"

She shook her head. "I want to see that young man. I'd know. But I don't see how it could really be Tommy."

"A good many people would have the knowledge to pass on to him, so he could convince Mrs. Traxler," said Jesse.

And Gilchrist said bluntly, "You'd have been able to do that, wouldn't you, Miss Drake? To tell him the kind of things that Tommy might remember."

"Me?" She looked scandalized. "You think I'd do a thing like that, just so somebody could get money from her? I don't know why you'd think I'd do such a thing! I was right good and angry with her at the time, as I had a right to be, and fond of Tommy as the rest of them were too, we all felt it, but none of us there then would do such a wicked thing—as fond of Tommy as we all were. I've got on all right in life, and Miss Beatrice is going to buy me a thing called an annuity, so I'll always have enough to live on even if I get too old to work. But that'll be a far day, I've always kept my health, knock wood, and unless Miss Beatrice drives me out of my mind with her scatty ways, I'll go on doing fine. She says, I'll have a quiet dinner alone, she says, and then coming in at six with a crowd of people and wanting a four-course dinner in an hour—scatty she is—but she's a cheerful body to have about and we rub along well enough. I've no need to go behind people's backs doing a thing like that just for money, and where'd I find such a young fellow who could pretend to be Tommy? Miss Beatrice doesn't know many young people, and about the only time I get out of this place is to go to the market." She gave them a fierce stare. "I don't know one thing about all this—only I'd like to see that young man."

Jesse and Gilchrist descended the stairs in silence and walked down to the Mercedes at the curb. Jesse said, "Verdict?"

"Oh, she sounds very damned plausible. Typical," said Gilchrist. "I just had one little thought. That very last thing she said."

"What about it?"

"The Ogilvie woman. She's no spring chicken as Clock said, and maybe her intimate friends aren't young. But she moves in theatrical circles, and I seem to remember reading somewhere that she's interested in aspiring young actors and actresses. And Jerry Smith's putting on a damned smooth performance, isn't he? The Drake woman could have met him casually when he came to that apartment to see Miss Ogilvie, and had the bright idea, and suggested it to him."

"Yes," said Jesse, "I see what you mean. Somehow I don't think it's quite as simple as that, but it's an idea."

* * *

On Thursday morning Gil Allen came into the office at eleven-thirty. Jesse was on the phone talking to the client about the divorce settlement, and waved him to a chair. When he put the phone down ten minutes later Allen was leaning back in the chair with his eyes closed, smoking quietly. He was the same little mousy terrier of a man, a trifle grayer, in an inconspicuous wrinkled gray suit; he would blend into backgrounds.

"I'll tell you, Mr. Falkenstein," he said, "I think you're wasting your money on paying us to shadow this principal of yours. Like I told Garrett. This is one hell of an offbeat thing, but by what you give us, the deal's set up, the mark's been roped and tied, and he won't be meeting with anybody who might be behind him."

"No, I'll agree with you there," said Jesse. "But you said to Garrett, he must be feeling damned bored. Having to keep the old lady sweet, keep his nose clean. And he told us he had been living in San Francisco recently, but he grew up in this area and he must have a few friends somewhere around, who know him as Jerry Smith. Sooner or later, if he gets bored enough, he may contact one of them—he strikes me as a gregarious young fellow. And it's very possible indeed that he couldn't resist telling an old pal about the soft spot he's landed in."

"I get you," said Allen. "It's possible."

"And we might lean on the pal a little, knowing who he is, and find out just what Jerry Smith might have told him."

"Yeah," said Allen. "Two plus two. I get you. I just didn't want to waste your client's money following him around to bars and old movies. I got to tell you that I lost him last night. Just for an hour or two."

"Oh. Where?"

"He was tooling around downtown. Sleazy old residential area. You know the parking situation. He caught me by surprise, he pulled into an empty slot on the street—it was Fourteenth Street—and there wasn't another in four blocks. I found a spot finally and went back. This was about eight-thirty, and he came back to the car about nine-thirty, but hell, by the time I got to my car he was long gone. But I think he went right back to the house, because when I got up there the Chrysler was in the drive. There's a three-car garage, but both the housekeeper and the chauffeur have their own heaps. Did anybody tell you she's got a Caddy?"

"Expectable. Are the other operatives collecting anything?"

"I couldn't say."

"Well, you carry on and we'll keep our fingers crossed."

"O.K. I'd better go see if Junior's ready to make a move. Another movie, or a nice ride down to the beach."

Jesse watched him out amusedly, and decided to go out to an early lunch. He had tried calling the Kendall house last night and got no answer. When he got back from lunch he tried again, with the same result. But just after the client left at five, he tried again and this time a woman answered. "Is Mr. Kendall there?"

"Just a moment, please."

"Kendall here," said a deep pleasant voice.

Jesse introduced himself. "Mr. Bradshaw at the Bureau office in Hollywood suggested I should contact you, Mr. Kendall. It's something to do with an old case you might be able to give me some information on."

"Well, you know, we aren't encouraged to hand out information on cases old or new to just anybody, Mr. Falkenstein."

"I realize that, but I think you'll see some reason on this one. I'd like to see you and talk it over anyway."

"Well, all right. I'll be glad to help you if I can."

"What about tonight?"

Kendall hesitated and said, "I'll tell you, I am bushed—we just got back an hour ago, had a long drive from Bakersfield. I'd just as soon have an early night. I'm just beginning to realize I'm not as young as I used to be. Can you make it about one tomorrow?"

Jesse laughed. "Hang on a minute." He consulted his desk calendar. Jean had an appointment listed at two o'clock, but it was with Dorheimer and he knew what it was about. Dorheimer was an old client, and he wanted to make a new will; his wife had died last month. He was a retired stockbroker and his time was his own. Jesse said to Kendall, "That'll be fine, thanks. See you then." He put the phone down and went out to the waiting room. "Jimmy, get hold of Dorheimer and apologize, tell him something's come up and we'll have to change his appointment to Monday. Any time that suits him."

He got home a little early; the gale had finally died down, and he found Nell busy with the trowel at the edge of the back yard, where the lawn gave way to the half-acre of tall old eucalyptus trees, busily tidying up her bed of bulbs. "What are you doing out here at this hour? It's nearly dark." Davy was happily prancing around the lawn with Athelstane.

"I know, I know. I was just going in, I can hardly see what I'm doing anyway. Everything's under control, there's a meat loaf in the oven and the salad's already made. Come on, Davy, time to go in."

Davy suddenly discovered that Daddy was home and made a beeline for him. "Daddy! Read about Mama Hubbard!"

"All right, big boy, come on in." And Jesse remembered the

little boy lost, gone all those years long back, and gave Davy an extra hard hug so that he squealed in protest. Athelstane bumbled along behind them to the back door. Murteza, being possessed of superior feline intelligence, was already in out of the chilly night air, ensconced in one of his favorite places on the mantelpiece. "There's a fire laid, if you want to light it," said Nell, stripping off her gardening gloves. "It's going to get colder."

* * *

He got some paper work done in the morning, had an early lunch and got out to the house in Encino at exactly one o'clock. Kendall was waiting for him, introduced him politely to his nice-looking gray-haired wife, took him down the hall to a paneled den. He might be retired, but he still bore the unmistakable stamp of the Bureau; the typical Fed, bland and tailored and courteous. He was wearing sports clothes but the effect was the same. He looked about sixty-five or a bit more, a tall lean man with thin gray hair, rather an intellectual face, intelligent gray eyes.

"Well, what's it all about, Mr. Falkenstein?" he asked. "Sit down. Cigarette?"

Jesse started to tell him in some detail. "I don't know if you remember the Traxler kidnapping at all, but evidently you were at the Hollywood Bureau at the time. Well—"

"Traxler," said Kendall. He smoothed one hand over his face. "Oh, yes. What about it?"

Jesse told him. "You can see the position," he said, when he'd outlined the case. "The thing's completely up in the air. We can be pretty sure that Jerry Smith is just Jerry Smith, and somebody with the necessary knowledge primed him to pull the con game on Mrs. Traxler, but so far there's no sort of proof, one way or the other."

"Yes," said Kendall. "It's an offbeat one, new to me, but it wouldn't be once in a blue moon this particular set of circumstances offered the opportunity. If you can get some proof, it'd be a felony charge. But I don't see how I can help you in any way."

"You fellows are always so damned close-mouthed," said Jesse. "Sometimes of necessity, I know. And you don't tell everything to the press at any time. We just heard something to the effect that you were pretty sure the Traxler boy was murdered. If you can give me something to back that up—"

Kendall smoothed his clean-shaven cheek again, ruminating. "Traxler," he said. He got up, went to stand at the window looking out into the side yard. "It's a hell of a time back," he said. "Yes, I was on that, with most of the other agents at the Hollywood Bureau. That was a bastard to work. I remember the case very well, partly because of that."

"I've got a little idea you boys knew more about it than got into the *Times*."

Kendall came back and sat down, got out another cigarette and lit it. "That's usually the case," he said, with a dry smile. "Yes, and we couldn't do one damn thing about it. You said up in the air. So was that one. We had a lot of ideas, but no real handle on it, and the only reason for that—we always suspected —was that the father hadn't cooperated all the way."

"Traxler?" said Jesse, astonished. "What the hell?"

"Oh, he was concerned—he was scared as hell, and that was why. Maybe too scared. When we came to look at it in depth— which is a thing we like to do—there was this and that showed up that could have tied that snatch right close to home."

"The inside job," said Jesse. "That ladder—"

Kendall waved an impatient hand. "I'm not talking about an inside job. There was a lot of damned guff in the press about that ladder. Naturally the snatchers were going to case the job, and they'd see it was there available. And as for somebody having inside information as to which window belonged to the child's room, hell, anybody with a cheap pair of binoculars could have spotted it—the curtains showed from outside, and they were bright yellow with circus animals printed all over them."

"Oh," said Jesse.

"Naturally we had a look at the servants and their associates, and it was pretty obvious right off that none of them could have had anything to do with it. I'm not talking about Traxler's home, I'm talking about his business. It was a very damned nice business, making him a lot of money. You heard how it got started during the Depression, started booming in the war with goverment contracts. He was still getting a lot of government contracts, defense stuff—it was small aircraft parts—mainstay of the firm. By the time of the kidnapping, he was employing about a thousand people, counting the office staff. And he'd been having trouble with the union. There was a company union, and their current contract was up and they were asking for a lot of new fringe benefits and other goodies. And then there were the Carnahans."

"And who were the Carnahans?" asked Jesse.

"Pair of brothers—Frank and Pat Carnahan—firebrand Socialists and you could say small-time agitators. They both worked at Traxler Precision Products. Frank was the head of the machine shop, and they'd got themselves elected as the top representatives of the company union. They'd been after the other union members, trying to argue them into joining a national union, but hadn't quite sold them on that one yet." Kendall was smoking reflectively, eyes on the spiral of smoke as it drifted toward the ceiling. "In fact, they'd just held another vote on that, and the majority had decided to stay with the company union. And Traxler—who was the sole owner of the business—was holding out against the union's demands. There'd been negotiations going on for a month before the kidnapping."

Jesse said interestedly, "You tied that in? Adding it how?"

"We didn't have to add it, for God's sake. It stuck out all over Traxler. We're used to dealing with the parents on a snatch—not, thank God, that they happen all that often. We got the idea that that was tied in early in the case. As soon as we were called on it we put a tap on the Traxler phones, at the house and at his office, and of course we were looking at the incoming mail, both places. The ransom demand could have come to either place, and we'd asked Traxler to go to his office every day—he didn't want to, but on that he cooperated. And of course it'd be very easy to slip him a message at the plant, either verbal or hand delivered. That we never heard about. We could have made the educated guess what it was. Play it straight like a good boy, hand over the ransom, but also, you'd better knuckle down to the union or you'll never see your son again."

"The Carnahans?" said Jesse. "Did they have any record?"

"No, they weren't pros in any sense of the word. But Traxler wouldn't let us mark the ransom money. The demand was for small-denomination unmarked bills—it always is—and he insisted on sticking by that. Claimed he didn't believe we could mark the money so it didn't show, and we'd be putting the child in danger. He wouldn't let the money out of his sight after he got it at the bank."

"That was a fairly smart idea they had, how to collect the ransom."

Kendall laughed shortly. "Fairly. There was one hell of a crowd at Santa Anita that day, we had a dozen men spotted around the pari-mutuel windows, but one minute Traxler had that briefcase, the next minute it was gone, and it could have changed hands a couple of times before it got outside the racetrack."

"Naturally, no sign of the Carnahans."

"Naturally. They could have hired a couple of small-time thugs, but I don't think that was necessary. There were some of those union members who thought the Carnahans were great big heroes about to lead the exploited workers out of the toils of the wicked capitalists. It's always dangerous to have too many people on a caper, but the Carnahans could have given a couple like that any story—nothing had come out about the snatch yet. But the point I wanted to make, the day before the ransom got paid, Traxler caved in to the union and agreed to the new contract without any compromises."

"Suggestive."

"As hell," said Kendall. "And you could put it down to his worry over the child—nothing else mattered."

"And they never got the child back, even so."

"No, and that finished Traxler. He just gave up. We kept an eye on the situation just for the hell of it, and the following year he sold the business, lock, stock and barrel to a national outfit who'd approached him about a merger before. And at that time the company union got dissolved and all the employees joined a national union."

"All right," said Jesse abruptly, "what about that body?"

Kendall stabbed out his latest cigarette and sighed. "Oh, yes, that body. All of us had the gut feeling it was the Traxler boy, but there wasn't a chance of positive identification. For one big starter, it was buried naked. Now that says somebody was smart. The forensic boys could do some miracles, even back then, and often enough a body's been identified by even shreds of clothes. The boy was wearing pajamas bought at a high-priced specialty shop, the label would have given that away. But for another thing, there was the place."

"Mission Canyon Park. I don't know it."

Kendall got up, rummaged and found a county guide in the bookcase. "It may be just another educated guess, and of course we hadn't any way to know where the kidnappers might have been heading when they got away with the kid. But—" He put the open county guide on Jesse's lap and stood behind the chair, bending to turn the pages. "Look at it. We don't know where they were heading, they could have been going south into Hollywood—the Carnahans both lived in Burbank—but here's Mulholland Drive, heading up into the foothills from the Mt. Olympus Estates. You know where it goes and how long it is." He flipped over pages to another map. "Right along the top of the foothills, the easiest access to a dozen roads leading into the San Fernando Valley. Past all the Valley towns, Burbank and on. And right here"—his blunt forefinger stabbed to the fourth map he had flipped to—"is Mission Canyon Park. It was just getting called that then. It was a land-fill area right off Mulholland just the other side of Sherman Oaks."

"I see. You thought—a handy place."

"A hell of a lot more than that. There wasn't one damned piece of evidence that that was the Carnahans, maybe with one of the wives to take charge of the kid—they were both married—that they picked up the kid, slapped a pad saturated with chloroform over his face and got him away quick and easy, and right away got onto Mulholland, the easiest route leading into the Valley. But that's what it could have looked like."

Jesse thought suddenly of what Margaret Niland had said. Not the narrow residential streets of Mt. Olympus—a curving steep road, and that described Mulholland—there'd be lights part way along it now, but not back then.

"And they hadn't gone far enough to turn off for Burbank, before they found the kid was dead. If that's where they were heading, of course. It happens. It happens all too easy sometimes. In the average snatch, where the kid winds up dead, it's accidental. They'd used a little too much chloroform, or used it too long. And they sat there in the dark arguing about what to do, and what they did do just came naturally. They followed Mulholland out to the nearest place they could dig a quiet grave —everywhere else along there it's steep hillside with thick underbrush—and that spot was already cleared, getting filled in. And maybe it was just getting light enough so they could see what they were doing. It was a lonely spot twenty-one years ago."

"Yes," said Jesse. "The body turned up more or less by accident?"

"They were shifting dirt around, making space for more fill." Kendall went back and sat down in his chair. "I saw Traxler myself, and told him we were pretty sure it was the boy. That was six months or so later. He wasn't much shocked or surprised—we all knew the boy had to be dead."

"And the other boy—"

"That one was probably picked up by a pervert—we talked to the local police about it. He was a little older than the Traxler boy. He never showed up anywhere, but even in a city, places a body can be hidden and never found. There's just an outside chance the body was his—all the doctors could say, it was a male child probably between five and six, and it conformed ap-

proximately to the size of the Traxler boy, but there wasn't anything definite."

"Ninety-nine percent," said Jesse thoughtfully.

"But what you say about Mrs. Traxler, do you think she'd believe it? Her husband probably tried to tell her then."

"Yes," said Jesse, "but it's something to go on with."

Kendall said cynically, "I see you have to do your best for a
client, the one cheated out of the money. But aside from that, I'd
say let the damned thing go—forget it. The old lady's enjoying
herself imagining she's got her boy back, and the father's in his
grave."

6

Gil Allen called his office at ten o'clock on Saturday morning. "I tried your house and your wife said you were doing some overtime at the office. He broke the pattern last night, Mr. Falkenstein. He met a girl and took her to dinner."

"Interesting," said Jesse. "Where did they go?"

"A fancy restaurant on La Cienega. Then they just went back to her pad. He left there about midnight and went home. I came back this morning to try to find out something about her. It's an old apartment on Carlton Way, and her name is June Brock. I pulled the old one on the manageress, asking for an insurance company, and she works at a drugstore on the Boulevard, she's lived there about four years, satisfactory tenant. I don't know how you want to play it, thought I'd check."

"Leave it for the time being. I've got a little idea that may change the situation some."

"However you want to play it."

"I'll get back to you." Jesse put the phone down and turned back to Charlene Garland. He had just started to talk to her when Allen called. "The reason I asked you to come in to see me, Mrs. Garland, is that I wanted to make it clear that we may never get anything definite enough to bring the con game home to him."

"I see, I was afraid of that."

"I don't want to waste your money for nothing. But on the other hand, there are possibilities here. I've got something else up my sleeve that may make a difference. All I wanted to ask you, do you want me to go on with this a while longer and see if we can come up with something? It's up to you."

She looked at him unhappily. She was wearing a gray tailored suit today with a white blouse and looked smart and attractive. "I think I do," she said slowly. "Probably it's no good for me—for us. I mean, Aunt Ruth's so annoyed at me now, even if we could prove to her he's not Tommy, she'd probably make a new will and leave everything to charity or something. But the whole thing makes me so mad, that—that actor getting money out of her and laughing at her behind her back, I'd just like to see him get what's coming to him, if that's possible. I'd like to find out—even if nobody can do anything about it—who planned all this, masterminded it."

Jesse went to stand by the window and looked down at the stretch of Wilshire Boulevard four stories below. He said, "I don't think it happened that way at all, Mrs. Garland."

"What do you mean?"

"I think the way it happened, the way it had to happen, it all started with Jerry Smith. Because he was Jerry Smith, with that particular background. I think somebody who knows your aunt, and all about that household and Tommy, ran into Mr. Smith quite casually and heard about his background—the orphanage, and how he never knew who he was or where he came from. And in the course of talk said casually that must have been about the same time as that kidnapping—and the idea just grew from there. That nobody would ever be able to prove that Jerry Smith wasn't Tommy, because of the background, and the somebody could pass on all the information so he sounded genuine. I think it's very possible that it just started out as an idle idea—I wonder if you could put it across—and once they started kicking it around, the money got more and more tempting."

"I can see that, of course it would have to be somebody like him, that nobody could trace back, prove he was somebody else. But, Mr. Falkenstein, if that's so, the other one would expect a share of the money. Wouldn't Jerry Smith be meeting him to hand it over, or mailing it to him, and that would be a way—"

"Not necessarily," said Jesse. "Uncle Sam is pretty jealous about anybody tampering with the mail, and we've got a tail on Mr. Smith, but so far he hasn't led us anywhere significant. It could be he's using the mail, yes. But also it would be a long-range deal, the casual chicken feed handed over now, pending a lump sum settlement on your aunt's death."

She said in a horrified tone, "You don't think he's planning to murder her?"

Jesse laughed. "No, I don't think that. But you said she has a bad heart. Just how bad, do you know?"

"Not really. She's been on some medication for years, I think it's something to do with an irregular heartbeat. She had an attack about ten years ago and was in the hospital quite a long time. She has to be careful about climbing stairs and walking too much, or so she says. I don't know if the doctor told her that or not."

"I see. Well, Mr. Smith—or the somebody—may have the idea that she could drop down dead at any minute. And I'd make a bet that she's already made a will leaving him a bundle, and that he knows it, and that, furthermore, that canny old boy Holden has drawn it up tight so there'd be no loopholes."

"What do you mean?"

"Well, you see, if she just left it 'to my son, Thomas Traxler, Jr.,' we could challenge it on the grounds that he's no such thing, she only thought he was. But if it's worded something like, 'to the person formerly known as Jerry Smith now known to me as my son, Thomas Traxler, Jr.,' etc., it'd probably be incontestable. Be one hell of a mess to try to contest it. And then there's a possibility that Holden—let's not make him the villain of the piece —did try to draw it up the first way because he knows it's a con game as well as we do, and she knew enough to stop him. She may be sentimental and foolish about the darling boy, but she might know enough for that."

"Uncle Tom always tried to see that she knew about business

matters, about the estate, he was ten years older and knew he might die first."

"Well, there you are."

"What are you going to do now?"

"Well, if anything can ever be proved, it would be a felony charge, Mrs. Garland. Obtaining money under false pretenses. If you're willing to lay a formal complaint with the police, we might rope them in to help."

"And what good would that do?"

"Oh, it's always handy to have the police on your side."

"Anything you think I should do—all right. I'd just like to see him get what he deserves, if that's possible."

"Oh, so would I. And maybe we're both thinking about it for the same reason, Mrs. Garland. There's a quotation from Voltaire— 'One owes respect to the living, but to the dead one owes nothing but the truth.' Tommy seems to have been a nice little boy."

Her eyes suddenly filled with tears. "Oh, yes, he was. Just the little I remember, such a funny shy little boy—and the absurd way she would have him stand up in front of people, so stiff and solemn, and recite the little pieces—"

"Yes. A nice little boy. Not very nice what happened to him." And he was thinking about the Carnahans, the company union, all the fringe benefits—and the little boy who might have been, at least for a brief time, so bewildered and frightened in the black night, adult motives and greed and cruelty swirling about him until merciful darkness came down.

"Anything you think I should do," she said dully. She stood up. "You'll let me know what happens."

"I'll let you know."

•   •   •

He got to the Hollywood station half an hour later, and found Clock and Petrovsky typing reports in the otherwise empty communal office; Gilchrist had preempted another detective's desk and was studying his notebook gloomily, chain-smoking. Jesse perched one hip on the corner of Clock's desk and said, "Busy?"

"Too busy," said Clock. "Things coming right and left. All the damned heisters—and this goddamned forgery ring stepping up operations—that redhead, we'll never get anywhere on her, she seems to have been a loner—all Nevada's turned up, she was living with some man, nobody seems to know his name, and he walked out on her. She may have been here just on a little vacation—"

Petrovsky said, "That address she had on her. That Jeff Gerard. He wouldn't have been the boyfriend, he'd been here at least six months, but maybe she thought he knew where the boyfriend was."

"Maybe, but we'll never know now. We put that damn senseless homicide in Pending, but the way things are going something new is going to go down any minute."

"You may be busier," said Jesse. "I think I'd like you in on this thing officially."

Clock groaned. "How?"

"Well, it would amount to a felony charge. Mrs. Garland is willing to lay a formal complaint."

"That's damned ephemeral, presumption of a crime already committed. Oh, I see it. You'd have to talk to the Captain about that."

"Yes—what I came in to do."

Gilchrist had been listening interestedly. "I don't see what good that'd do you."

Jesse said gently, "Andrew's always an asset at leaning on people—the big tough cop—he can scare witnesses a lot easier than I could."

"What witnesses?" asked Clock sourly.

"Well, we've got a new one to look at anyway. Is the Captain in?"

Clock said exasperatedly, "I'll go and see."

Jesse spent three quarters of an hour with Captain Kelsey, who listened to the story glumly and agreed that there was something in it for official investigation. "You understand, we can't spend too much time on a thing like this, Falkenstein, the on-going urgent crimes of violence we've got to cope with.

When I think what a nice clean town this was when I first made rank—" he sighed. "The place seething with pimps and hookers these days, an average of four heists a night, my God." He looked tired. "But that's a sweet con game, and if Clock can give you some help on it, fine. Only he'd better not neglect anything else."

Jesse took Clock and Gilchrist out for a belated lunch and passed on the latest aspects of the Traxler thing. "This girl—" said Clock.

"Yes," said Jesse. "Reason I told Allen to hold off, I wanted you on hand to scare her with your ugly mug."

"Maybe we'll get somewhere now," said Gilchrist in satisfaction.

"Don't get your hopes up. We may not, too."

"Which drugstore?" asked Clock resignedly.

"Thrifty on Hollywood Boulevard. I don't think you need to bring her in for questioning at the station until we know more."

"Hell," said Clock, "do a little overtime and try to catch her at the apartment? All right, I'd better call Fran. But I can't say I'm sorry you brought us into it, it's a teasing little business—and a hell of a lot more refined than dealing with the heisters and homicides. I've been telling Gilchrist, he'll never get an interesting book out of day-to-day police work. It's too damned monotonous, same things day in day out, the crude violence and plain damned foolishness."

"You'd be surprised at the kind of thing nice people like to read, Sergeant," said Gilchrist sardonically. "It's a contrast to their nice safe suburban lives."

"And not so damned safe these days at that," said Clock, massaging his jaw. "The burglary rate's way up too."

*　*　*

Jesse and Clock were waiting at the Carlton Way apartment at six o'clock when June Brock came home. Clock had talked to the manager at the drugstore and verified that the day shift was eight to five, and they'd heard from the apartment manageress that she didn't have a car.

The apartment was an old and shabby one. It would have been here since the twenties, on this side street in the heart of central Hollywood that was run down and slatternly now. June Brock's apartment was on the second floor at the rear, and as she came down the dark hall she didn't see them until she was nearly at the door. She had her key out, and shied back at the sight of two tall men, one lean and one broad, in the hallway so near. She bent to the door and Clock said, "Miss Brock?"

She shied again, nervously. "Yes?" she said.

Clock had his badge out. "LAPD," he said tersely in his deep voice. "We'd like to ask you a few questions if you don't mind."

She looked scared. She was in the mid-twenties, with defiantly golden hair down to her shoulders and a shallowly pretty face plastered with too much makeup; she still had on her yellow uniform from the drugstore, with a shabby navy coat over it. "Cops," she said, looking at the badge. "Questions about what? I haven't done anything."

"We never said you did," said Clock cheerfully. "Can we go in?"

She unlocked the door and they went in after her; she reached automatically to switch on the overhead light. It was the typical tired furnished apartment of its period. In the living room, small and square, were a few pieces of ancient furniture, overstuffed couch and chair faded to no color, a newer platform rocker, a black-and-white TV in one corner. There was a glimpse one way into a narrow kitchen with a metal table and two chairs at this end, the other way into a bedroom.

"What do you want with me?" she asked in a frightened voice. She'd had a better look at Clock in the light and she didn't like him at all.

"Just a few questions. You were out on a date last night, weren't you?"

She nodded reluctantly.

"We'd like to ask you about the fellow you dated."

She was surprised at that. "Is Jerry in any trouble?"

"He could be," said Jesse. "That's his name, Jerry? Jerry what?"

"Jerry Smith. He's a nice guy. I don't see how he could be in any trouble with cops."

"How long have you known him?" asked Clock. "Where'd you meet him?"

"What is all this, anyways? Jerry wouldn't be in any cop trouble. I've known him about three months. I met him at the place I work—"

"The drugstore on Hollywood Boulevard?" said Clock.

"That's right. I'm at the tobacco counter, he came in to buy cigarettes and we got talking, you know how you do. He seemed like a nice guy, we sort of hit it off, and he asked me for a date. We aren't going steady or anything, he just calls me once in a while and we have a date."

"Or anything?" said Clock genially. "What's that amount to?"

She flushed angrily. "It's a girl's own damn business what she does or doesn't do with a boyfriend. It's nothing to do with you."

"All right, what do you know about him? Does he have a job?"

"I don't get all this, he was out of a job when I first met him, but I guess he's got a pretty good one now, he gets to drive a brand new car, a real classy one, and the last few times we've gone to real nice places."

"You don't know what kind of a job?" asked Jesse.

"Well, just that he works for an old lady, he said it's a real good spot, easy work. I guess he drives her around and like that. Like a chauffeur. Listen, he's a perfectly honest guy, he wouldn't be up to anything wrong, a girl can tell, you know."

"You think so?" said Jesse. He looked at Clock sadly. Clock shrugged. "That's all you can tell us?"

"That's all anybody could tell you about Jerry. He's just a guy, a nice guy—and he's not the only boyfriend I got. I said we weren't going steady—it's nothing serious between us, just a little fun. What the hell do you think Jerry's done?"

"You don't know who the old lady is?"

She looked bewildered now. "Now how the hell would I? He never said her name, what's the difference? You cops—"

"And I suppose you'll let him know we were asking questions," said Clock.

She said hotly, "You bet I'll let him know next time he calls me—I don't have a number for him, he said he can't use the phone at the old lady's house."

"All right, all right," said Clock. "That's about all we wanted to ask, isn't it?" He looked at Jesse. They left her staring after them angrily.

They'd come in Clock's Pontiac. They got into the front seat and lit cigarettes. "Damn all," said Clock.

Jesse said mournfully, "Natural taste of Mr. Smith, the common pickup, the cheap little blonde. We said he was getting bored. He just wanted some female company, and that was available. I can see him introducing that one to Mrs. Traxler as his girl friend."

"And of course she doesn't know a damn thing," said Clock. "What have your private eyes turned up, anything? And don't expect us to take over for them."

"I don't know."

"You always like to exercise your imagination. Are you having any bets at all on who's behind Smith?"

"Maybe there are too many possibilities altogether—it's anybody's guess, Andrew. I'd like the nursemaid for it, for a couple of reasons. The things he came out with, to convince Mrs. Traxler, are the exact things the nurse might hand him out of her fond memories. The things she remembers best. And Gilchrist could be right that she might have run across Smith in the crowd around Bea Ogilvie. But there are other things against it. Anybody in that crowd would be at least casually known to a good many people, maybe as an aspiring young actor. The nurse could well have held that grudge, but she's a simple sort of character, Andrew, I don't see her as imaginative enough to get the idea of pushing the ringer onto Mrs. Traxler. What I do think is that there is no connection at all showing on the surface between Mr. Smith and whoever handed him the information. There couldn't be—there mustn't be. They couldn't have known that there wouldn't be some sort of investigation of Mr. Smith—even if not on Mrs. Traxler's part, how could they know her lawyers would take that cynical attitude, not go scurrying around trying to prove he couldn't be Tommy? If it's one of the servants, they'd know about the only relative, Charlene Garland—that it was unlikely she'd accept him at face value."

"Then how did they get together?"

"I've got no idea," said Jesse. "It could have been—it probably was—the very casual thing, friend of friends. I don't know."

"Well, I suppose all these servants have private lives too. If your private operatives can get at them." Clock started the engine. "This was a damned waste of time."

"But it shows that Mr. Smith is bored all right. I still say he has to have some old pals round about, and what's the good of falling into a nice soft spot with all the money if you can't do a little boasting about it? He may be canny enough not to let out the whole story to anybody, but—and there is, as Mrs. Garland reminds us, the money. Whatever the source was, there's bound to be a split agreed on. If it was one of these old servants, he or she wouldn't be helping him onto that lay just for the satisfaction of putting over a fast one on Mrs. Traxler. We don't know what kind of money she's handing out, but Mrs. Garland guessed, and I guessed too, a regular allowance—that'd be the natural thing, wouldn't it?"

"Probably."

"And expectations to come. She's not a young woman and she's said to have a bad heart. Mrs. Garland doesn't know how bad. I told you what I think about the will."

Clock said consideringly, "So much down and a lump sum to come."

"It could be—again the natural thing. He may be paying over so much a month, and the easiest way to do it would be by mail, and that we'd have no way of tracking down. Even if you persuaded Uncle Sam to let you have a look, no go. It'll be the plain envelope with no return address, and cash inside, mailed at an anonymous box on the street."

"And when she dies," said Clock softly, "the bigger split."

"Yes, naturally."

"There's no way to get at it, for God's sake. You may as well admit it, Jesse."

"Don't say so, Andrew. We may get a break. One thing you ought to know from all your experience, the crooks are only smart up to a point. Sometimes they're too smart nine tenths of the way, and then they pull some damn stupidity that gives away the whole show."

"That's so," said Clock. "I'd like to know the answer on this one, but right now it doesn't look likely we ever will. Well, thanks for nothing." He pulled up in the parking lot of the office building on Wilshire. "I'm starving and Fran's mad at me, she had something special for dinner that wouldn't keep."

"You ought to train her to be a more dutiful wife," said Jesse.

* * *

On Sunday morning he had just finished looking at the paper and Nell was out working in the yard again, when the phone rang. A crisp businesslike female voice said, "Mr. Falkenstein? Mary Lester of Garrett Associates. Mr. Garrett asked us to report directly to you. I don't know what you'll think of what I've got, but I thought you'd like to hear it. Would you like me to come to the house?"

"Fine, I'd better tell you how to get here, we're a little isolated—"

"I looked it up in the county guide. I'll be there in fifteen minutes."

When she came, driving an old tan Ford, she turned out to be a thin dark woman in her forties, her not unattractive face innocent of much makeup, her plain dark brown blouse and skirt neither smart nor dowdy. She let him take her coat and accepted a cigarette, sitting down on the couch. "Nice house," she said. "You must get a lot of fresh air up here above the city."

Jesse apologized for Davy's toys and the Sunday paper strewn over the floor and she waved a careless hand. "Looks lived in. I've got a three-room cell over on Las Palmas—I miss the beach, used to live in Santa Monica." He felt momentary curiosity how

and why Miss Lester—she didn't wear a wedding ring—had
ended up as an operative for Garrett Associates; she was a
definite personality. Murteza deigned to leap down from the
mantel to investigate a stranger, and let her stroke him. "Nice
cat. Well, Mr. Falkenstein, I don't know what you'll think of
what I've got for you. This is an interesting case, very much
offbeat, isn't it? That housekeeper, Ingrid Goodman—Mr. Garrett said, decide for yourself how to go at it. A live-in servant
like that, it was a little difficult. Not just a matter of shadowing
her, because she hardly ever goes out. She went to the market
Monday and Wednesday, and each time she left about noon and
took herself to lunch at a coffee shop on Hollywood Boulevard—
maybe she gets tired of her own cooking. The second time I
thought about tackling her right there, it was crowded and I'd
probably have had the chance to sit at the same table. There
were several approaches I could have used. I thought of getting
her talking and telling her I was looking for a job and was thinking of trying domestic work for a change—ten to one she'd have
opened up and talked about her own job, you see. Only there
were a couple of things against that. I'd had a good look at her
by then—I did some shopping behind her at the market—and
she didn't look to me like a very forthcoming sort of woman, the
kind who talks much or easily. And then you never know when
it might be a disadvantage for a subject to be able to recognize
you."

"Very foresighted," said Jesse.

"You have to be, at this job. But I knew she'd have to have a
day off sometime, the usual rule is once a week. So I just parked
myself up there, round a corner out of sight, and waited until I
was sure she wasn't going out. I figured, on her day off she'd
probably get the old lady's breakfast and leave by nine-thirty or
so, you see. She didn't go out at all on Thursday or Friday, but
yesterday she left in her car about ten o'clock. She's driving an
old Chevy, by the way. She went downtown in Hollywood and
parked in a public lot—so did I—and went into the Broadway
Department Store. She shopped around for quite a while,
bought some children's clothes and toys, and then she had lunch

at the same coffee shop. I didn't dare go in and order, they were busy and I was afraid I'd lose her by being stuck in a rear booth."

"And I'll bet you could have stood some lunch by then too."

"Oh, well," said Miss Lester, lighting another cigarette, "all in the day's work and just as well for the figure. You get used to inconveniences. She went back to the car and drove way downtown in L.A. to San Marino Street. Of course there wasn't a parking place anywhere around, but I spotted the house she went to—she turned into the drive—and I found a public lot up on Hoover and moseyed on back there on foot. I was wondering just exactly how to play it—I could have made an excuse to ring the bell—"

"Insurance," said Jesse.

"Canvassing for a political candidate," said Miss Lester briskly, "or taking a survey of some sort—the gimmicks advertising companies can think up to waste people's time—but I still didn't want to meet the woman face-to-face, you see. That's a terribly run-down part of town now, you probably know, ramshackle old houses and dirty yards—some single houses, a few apartments—a real slum. I was wondering what on earth Mrs. Traxler's housekeeper was doing down there, when I had a little break. As I came up the block, I saw her come out on the front porch there, and some others with her—a youngish woman in a perfectly horrible bright pink coat—pure Main Street, not to say Skid Row—and three kids about seven down to three. Did I say it was one of the single houses? The young woman locked the front door and they all got in the housekeeper's car and drove off. So I could deduce that there wasn't anybody home. I went up and rang the bell in case any neighbors were watching, and then I tried the house on one side and nobody answered so I tried the other side. And the woman who answered the door was just the type we pray for in any investigation. A talker. She's a widow, a Mrs. Erwin, she lives alone and I suppose she's starved for anybody to talk to. My God, how that woman talked. I told her I was an insurance investigator looking for some information about the people next door—there was a name slot right beside

the mailbox, the name was the same as the housekeeper's, Goodman—and she said she wouldn't give those trashy folk any insurance if she was the company, they were no better than they
should be. Just riffraff, the children let to run wild, the neighborhood was running down something awful when people like
that moved into it and they weren't the only ones—so I heard all
about the woman four doors down who has men calling on her
at all hours, and Mrs. Erwin knows what to make of that, and
the couple across the street who get drunk and go to fighting
with each other in the front yard—once the wife chased him all
the way up the block with a carving knife, and Mrs. Erwin
wouldn't soil her lips by repeating what she was yelling at him—
and I maneuvered her back to the Goodmans and she said they
were no-good trash too, always getting behind in the rent, that
she knew for a fact because the same landlord owns the place
Mrs. Lloyd rents down the block, and Mrs. Lloyd is a friend of
hers—I gather, the only other decent respectable female on the
block—and he's told Mrs. Lloyd it was like pulling teeth to get
the rent out of them. And that reminded her of the people that
got evicted at the other end of the block, they were on welfare
and the welfare people tried to stop them getting evicted and in
the end the police had to be called, and it was the kind of thing
that didn't happen in a decent neighborhood. When she and her
husband started to buy the house it had been a nice quiet neighborhood, and he'd worked for the railroad so it was convenient
to get to the S.P. yards and likely he was turning in his grave
now that it was all nationalized—and I got her back to the
Goodmans and she said that no-good Robert Goodman was usually out of a job, when he did work it was just at gas stations and
like that, and the wife—if they were married and who knew
about that—sat around all day drinking beer and let the kids
run wild, they were always tramping through her flower bed in
the back yard—and sometimes they gave wild parties with a lot
of noisy young people whooping around and probably drunk—if
it wasn't these awful drugs they took—and that reminded her of
some teenager in the next block who'd been arrested for selling
dope and that just showed how the neighborhood was going, but

of course the house was paid for and she couldn't afford to move—and I steered her back to the Goodmans and she said they'd probably be on welfare if it wasn't for his mother, and the woman must be a fool to keep on throwing money away on them, they didn't appreciate it, but she must have a good job somewhere, she came every week and brought the kids presents and went out and bought groceries for them, and Mrs. Erwin knows for a fact—from Mrs. Lloyd, of course—that she's paid up the rent for them lots of times too. And it was a mystery because the mother looked to be a nice respectable woman, a cut above the rest of the family, a long way you could say, you'd think a decent woman would be ashamed of a son in jail—oh, yes, he'd been in jail a couple of times, and last year he'd been in for a long time, only got out last September."

Jesse had been hanging on her words, and now said, "Beautiful."

"I thought you'd like it," said Miss Lester modestly.

"Gas stations," said Jesse. "That's just exactly the kind of casual contact—nothing showing on the surface—Miss Lester, thanks. I'll see you get a bonus."

"It was just the breaks, Mr. Falkenstein. I hope it does you some good. I'd like to know the end of this case if it ever has one."

Before she pulled out of the driveway he was on the phone to Clock. Clock said in annoyance, "We just brought in a possible heister to question. Oh, hell, calm down and I'll see if we can spare you some time."

He couldn't until past one o'clock; Jesse spent the time talking to Gilchrist. They had a hasty lunch at the nearest coffee shop, and Clock took them down to Parker Center, Central Headquarters LAPD. There in that impressive pile, he led the way down to the labyrinth of Records and Information, and asked for the package on Robert Goodman. The pretty blond policewoman at the front desk went away and in five minutes came back with a couple of photocopied pages.

"Well, there you are," said Clock. "He's twenty-seven, a hundred and fifty, five-ten, black and brown—hell, that's not important. I'll lay you any money there's a juvenile record too, but we mustn't penalize the JD's chances in life by keeping that on file. Petty theft, grand theft, grand theft—possession of controlled drugs—and he's had, as per usual, the probation, the plea bargain, and he didn't serve any appreciable time in the slammer until last year. Another count of grand theft from his employer, and he got a one-to-three and served nine months. It's just the sort of contact we were thinking about—"

"Fond, doting mama," said Jesse. "Never tired of helping out sonny boy down on his luck. I like it. I like it very much. He'll have pals—who also worked at gas stations—and just occasionally mama meeting one when everybody's out of a job—and by God, that's something else that should have occurred to me, of course, but you can't think of everything—the Constable."

"The constable?" said Clock blankly. "A British bobby?"

"No, no, the painting over the mantel," said Jesse impatiently. "I should have realized that the source couldn't be one of those old servants, just because of that. When they were there, when Tommy was kidnapped, there was a reproduction of one of Constable's paintings over the mantel—then about five years ago Mrs. Traxler had the place redecorated and there's a different picture there now. And that was one of the points Jerry Smith told her about. And Mrs. Goodman knew about that."

"Oh, yes," said Clock. "So now we take a look at all Goodman's pals, and at least a few of them will tell us, sure, Bob Goodman knows Jerry Smith. It's just the sort of contact—"

"Look—look," said Gilchrist plaintively. "What I'd like to know, who had the idea of bringing my book into it? As the supposed trigger? None of these people sound like habitual readers to me."

"Possibly it was Mr. Smith's idea," said Jesse. "Yes, she hearing all about his anonymous background—and there's another psychological point, too. Two women alone in that house—and Mrs. Traxler is a talker. I'll bet the Goodman woman's got good and damned bored hearing all about Tommy and the kidnapping. And even something else—the carefully preserved nursery—Mrs. Traxler used to service most of her life, and it won't be her who keeps it clean and dusted. Mrs. Goodman'll be very familiar with that nursery, the stuffed bear and the rocking horse and the furry rug by the fireplace and the door into Judy's room."

"Prove the connection, it might be enough to make them both break down and admit it," said Clock, pleased.

"And he wouldn't have to use the post office to pay her her cut," said Jesse, "living in the same house. I think we'll leave the rest of this up to you, Andrew."

"Listen," said Gilchrist, "I'd just like to know where my book comes in."

"That's just a detail," said Clock.

* * *

On Monday morning at ten o'clock Jimmy came into Jesse's office and said, "You've got another visitor without an appointment. A Miss Drake."

Jesse looked up from where he'd been poring over figures for that divorce settlement. He said incredulously, "Drake? Well, O.K., I'll see her."

She came in slowly, a dowdy little fat woman in a shabby black coat, a queer old-fashioned felt hat, and he got up and offered her a chair. "I beg your pardon for coming without notice, sir." He wondered how old she was. An experienced nanny already when she came over with the English family attached to the Embassy; other jobs here before she went to Mrs. Traxler; in her late thirties then; perhaps, in her early sixties now.

"That's all right, Miss Drake, what did you want to see me about?"

She was looking miserable, the round face with its apple-red cheeks a little drawn and pinched. "I wanted to tell you, sir, that you were right," she said. "When you told me all that the other day, I just had to see that young man. I felt I'd know for certain sure if it was Tommy. And they were only *nearly* sure that Tommy was dead—it could be him. So I went up there on the bus—I don't drive—and it was an awful walk up that hill, but I got there. Oh, didn't it bring memories back, to see the house again! It was about two o'clock yesterday afternoon, and when I got there I didn't rightly know what to do—I didn't want to see Mrs. Traxler again, I didn't hardly like to ring the bell—but I wasn't there ten minutes before he came out. I knew it had to be that young man, and he started for a car in the driveway. And I just went up to him bold as brass and asked if a Mr. Jones lived there"—she took a breath—"and he smiled quite nice at me and said no, and got into the car—oh, sir, I thought if I could get close to him, I'd know for certain sure—a child I'd had all the care of since he was born—you'd think you'd know—but I didn't, sir. I don't know at all. He might be Tommy—or he might not. I just don't know." She looked at him pitiably.

7

All that looked as if the answer had fallen into their laps, but until and unless it seemed cut and dried, Jesse's innate caution prevented him from calling off the private eyes. You never knew, and another week of looking wouldn't do any harm. He didn't know what more they might turn up, but he felt reasonably justified when Clock called him on Friday afternoon. Clock was sounding harassed.

"The hell with the Captain," he said. "I wanted to get this cleared out of the way. I roped the Bunco squad at Headquarters in on it, twisted a few arms, they've got more men to turn loose on a case. And we haven't come up with one damned thing, Jesse, no smell of a Jerry Smith connected in any way with Robert Goodman. We've seen all his employers for five years back, none of them ever heard of a Jerry Smith, we've talked to most of his friends."

"You've been busy," said Jesse.

"Neglecting everything else at home base, damn it. There's no hint of a connection. It looked like the open-and-shut answer, but now where do we go? I think I'd like to tackle the woman direct, we might just make her come apart."

"I wonder," said Jesse.

"I'm going to catch her on her day off—tomorrow, Saturday— if we went to the house, it'd alert him that there's an investigation going on, and hell, it probably will anyway—he'll already have heard from the Brock girl that there are cops sniffing around."

"And maybe not, if he hasn't called her again."

"And I don't know that it would do any harm. He's been thinking he's got it made, well entrenched with fond mama—you haven't showed again, he probably thinks he convinced you, at least that you realize there's no way to oust him, and that the Garland woman's given up trying to do anything about it. It'll shake him to find us officially questioning Mrs. Goodman."

"It might not do any harm, no."

"I wondered if you'd like to sit in."

"I think I would, Andrew. Thanks. What's the agenda?"

"Evidently she usually gets to the place on San Marino in early afternoon—I'll be waiting and we'll take her into headquarters to talk to. You can meet me at the office at noon."

"Fair enough. But I wonder if this doesn't look too easy, Andrew. I've been having second thoughts about it."

"Damn it, it's the only answer, it's got to be. Well, I'll see you."

The reason Jesse had been having second thoughts was Gil Allen's written report. He hadn't got it until Tuesday, hadn't got around to looking it over until yesterday, thinking there probably wouldn't be much new in it anyway, but when he did, one little fact stood out clear and interesting. Subject, ran Allen's semi-official prose, left house at 1:00 P.M. Friday, drove to central Hollywood and had two drinks at Nikki's Bar on La Brea. Stopped on way back to car to mail letter in street box on corner. Proceeded to movie house on Vermont and took in first show, came back to house in Mt. Olympus 4:45. Jesse, reading that, looked backward and forward at the reports for different dates. Allen had had an eye on Jerry Smith for nearly three weeks now, and three times he had mailed a letter in a street box. The payoff to the source, weekly instead of monthly? And that wouldn't be Ingrid Goodman, living in the same house. That contact had looked so likely when it showed up, but he wondered. And in spite of the fact that Mr. Smith was obviously bored, he still hadn't contacted anybody but bartenders and ticket sellers at movie houses. Playing it very canny indeed. Jesse wondered if the money was worth it to him when it entailed such an aimless life. Well, it didn't have to stay that way. He was still entrenching himself with the woman—and she would be urging him to make friends among the younger generation of her friends—join the country club, occupy himself as a young moneyed gentleman should—and he playing it safe, not inclined for all that, but he might come to it eventually to please her. In fact, there were signs just in the last couple of days that he might be doing that. On Wednesday he had gone to the Beverly Hills Country Club and looked around, had a drink at the club-house bar, which was open to the public, and talked with the waiter at some length. Yesterday he had shopped for more new clothes at an exclusive men's store in Hollywood, and among other things bought a pair of golf shoes. Jesse cocked his head at the report. The honest transparent Mr. Smith had apparently given up the idea of entering the university to improve his education.

He met Clock at the Hollywood station at noon on Saturday and they drove down to San Marino Street. Clock said, "A fellow from Bunco'll meet us here—I thought it'd be easier to take her into Headquarters." The streets down here were ancient and dirty, the houses poor and ill kept, the blacktop broken and pitted. It was another gray cold day with a chilly wind.

The man from Central Headquarters was Novak, a pock-marked hard-bitten-looking middle-aged man who didn't talk much. They waited in Clock's car. There was an old heap of a Ford parked in the drive of the house. Novak said, "That's his. He's out of a job again. Held on just until he got off parole, that was last week, showed up late and then didn't show up at all and got fired. But you wanted to talk to the mother, not him."

"That's right," said Clock.

She drove up about one-thirty in the old Chevy, and they got out and approached her as she went up to the porch. She turned inquiringly at steps behind her as the front door opened.

"Ma, I got to ask you to lend me some rent money again—"

He stopped as he spotted the men behind her. He was a weedy young fellow with slicked-back long black hair and a prominent Adam's apple. Behind him in the house was the sound of children's voices arguing noisily.

"Mrs. Goodman?" said Clock. He held out the badge. "We have a few questions we'd like to ask you."

She looked more surprised than anything else. The flat Scandinavian face wouldn't show much emotion. "Me? What about? Police—" She turned to her son in the doorway, "You haven't been getting in trouble again, have you?"

"No, course not. I'm clean, they got no call bothering you. They just like to pick on people." He looked nervous. "You got no call pick on my mother, you cops."

Novak said, "Just a few questions, Mrs. Goodman, if you don't mind coming with us?"

"Questions about what?"

"Let's go back to Headquarters, ma'am."

She was silent on the short ride down to Parker Center, but looked uneasy, darting looks at Novak and Clock. There, they took her up to the Bunco office: as at the Hollywood station, there was a large communal detective office with a row of interrogation rooms down the hall, but they wouldn't all fit into one of those. Novak put her in a chair beside his desk, pushed up other chairs for Clock and Jesse. She said suddenly to Jesse, "I've seen you before. You came to the house—"

"That's right, Mrs. Goodman. Representing Mrs. Charlene Garland. Mrs. Garland and a few other people don't like to see Mrs. Traxler being defrauded of money by an imposter, and we're going to prove he's an imposter. He's not really her son, and you know that, don't you?"

She said, showing a little spirit, "I don't know that. Is this about that? About Mrs. Traxler, not Robert? I don't understand—"

"You understand all right," said Clock. "It was you gave him all the useful information so he could convince Mrs. Traxler he is her son, wasn't it?"

"I don't know what you're talking about."

"All the little facts about the contents of that nursery, and the picture over the mantel, and the little pieces Tommy used to recite—everything he told Mrs. Traxler."

"Why should I do that? No, I never told him anything."

"For all the money, Mrs. Goodman—so he could get the money from her."

"She's got a right to give him money if she wants, he's her boy."

"You know he's not. Her son is dead, he's been dead a long time. Smith is putting over a nice con game on her, and you helped him do it."

She said, suddenly fierce, "I never did such a thing! That other woman, she's the one told you all the lies and put you after him because she wants all the money herself—I heard what Mrs. Traxler said, hiring a crooked lawyer to try to show he's not her own son—do you suppose a mother wouldn't know? I don't know anything about the ins and outs of it, how he found out she's his mother and came back where he belongs—but she'd know, a mother'd always know in her heart, she'd know her own son whatever happened—you men wouldn't understand that, but it's so! Don't you think I've grieved right along with that poor woman, the times and times she's told me about losing him that awful way, she never forgot, a mother don't forget ever, and her keeping everything of his just as it was, his little playthings and all—don't you think I understood it and felt for her in my heart? We're both women. And she's a dignified lady, she's a real lady, but to the day I die I'll never forget how she said to me— she said to me"—her voice was shaking with emotion—"'I'd let him in, such a nice-looking young man, and she saw him in the living room, and then I heard her take him upstairs, I wondered, but I never thought—and she come to me in the kitchen, and she'd been crying, and, 'Ingrid,' she says, 'he's come back to me. My boy's come back to me, that's my Tommy!' And I was so flabbergasted I didn't know what to say, and I just said, 'Oh, madam,' like that—and she put her arm around me and began to cry again and I made her sit down because she was all gone a queer color and I knew her heart is bad—and she said, 'It's my Tommy, he's come back to me. Those cruel people put him in a terrible orphanage and he forgot who he was until just a little while ago'—and I never saw her look so happy—and my heart went right out to her, I said, 'Oh, madam, it's too good to be true,' I said, and she said, 'Ingrid, I couldn't go to church, I thought it must be all a lie about God being kind because I prayed so hard for Tommy to be safe and come back to me and it didn't happen—all those years, all the lonely years, and poor Tom gone without knowing he was safe, and now he's come back to me, it's too good to be true indeed'—my heart went out to her! Don't you think a woman'd feel for another woman? And now you're all trying to take him away from her—spoil the only happiness she's had in more than twenty years—"

Jesse said gently, "The real Tommy's dead, Mrs. Goodman."

"You can lay off the play acting," said Clock brutally, "we can read it, just how it happened. This Jerry Smith is a friend of your son's, isn't he? And that's where you met him, and heard about his growing up in the orphanage, and you had the bright notion how he could pass himself off as Tommy come back—you knew she'd never believed that Tommy was dead, she must have said that to you often, didn't she?"

"No, she never believed he was dead—she said, a mother would know—and I know that too, you'd know if your own flesh and blood was dead. My own boy, he hasn't maybe been as good as he ought to be, the way I tried to raise him after his father died, but your own flesh and blood you can't forget or turn your back on, and a mother'd know if he was dead. I believed her. She'd know. It doesn't matter what he told her or didn't tell her."

Clock said coldly, "And all this womanly sympathy just helped to fix the idea in her head, didn't it? Just as you knew it would."

"She was happy for the first time in all those years, and just because that other woman's jealous and wants the money instead, you'll try to take him away, make out he's some kind of criminal! It's all her put the idea in your heads—I heard what she said the day you come," and she looked at Jesse bitterly. "Getting hold of a crooked lawyer to try to prove she doesn't know her own son!"

Novak said tiredly, "It would be a serious charge, you know—defrauding the old lady—both of you could go to prison for that, maybe for a long time. We'll locate people who can tell us that you knew Jerry Smith, that you met him in your son's house, and that proves the connection—as Sergeant Clock says, you knew all the information to give him, to persuade the old lady, and that makes you as guilty as he is. But if you'll tell us all about it, open up and tell us just how it happened, we can get you off on a lesser charge and you may not go to prison at all. What about it?"

She said passionately, "You can put me in jail the rest of my life!" Had they thought the high-cheekboned face incapable of showing emotion? In a shaking voice she repeated, "The rest of my life! I'll never tell you nothing but what's so—I never saw him before in my life, I didn't know him, I never saw him till he came to the house that day—and I don't know what he said to her, it don't matter what he said to her—" Her grammar was slipping under stress. "What did it matter what he said to her, she knew he was her boy! After all those years—and she's been so happy—and just because that other woman wants all the money, you're trying to make out he's a crook of some kind! I can't tell you what you want me to because it's not so, I don't know nothing to tell! You take him away from her again and she'll just die, I know she would!"

Jesse touched Clock's arm, and they left her sitting there wiping her eyes with a handkerchief and went across the big room. "That sounds pretty damned genuine," said Jesse.

"Play acting," said Novak. "She's playing for time."

"I wonder," said Clock. "You know, everybody we've talked to, Robert Goodman's friends, employers, they all claim they never heard of a Jerry Smith. And it's just damn silly to say they'd all be in the know, even to the slight extent that Smith is on a crooked lay somewhere. They're all ordinary, typical. Goodman's the only one we've run across who's got a little pedigree. If he'd known Smith, we'd have heard about it from somebody."

"Well, you'd think so," said Novak. "But you were damned sure this was the connection you were looking for."

"It looked like it. It looked so good, so natural. What do you think, Jesse?"

"It doesn't look so good now, does it? All right, discount all the weeping and wailing if you like, but she's that sort of woman, Andrew—all feeling and not much common sense. All that sounds as if she means it."

Novak said, "Well, you've warned him now, anyway. I wonder what he'll do. Sit tight, there's nothing else he can do, and he's in a damned strong position and he knows it. If you ask me, this was a waste of time to try to work from the start. If you could nail down the connection—" He looked across at Mrs. Goodman and shook his head. "That's a damned obstinate female, and"—to Jesse—"I wouldn't just go along that she's got no sense. She's shrewd enough to know, if she just goes on saying all that, there's no action we can take. You'd have to prove the connection between Smith and the source of information to have anything concrete for a charge."

Clock said testily, "We've realized that all along, that's what makes this such a bastard to work. I don't know that I'll go on thanking you, Jesse, for getting us involved in the damned thing. When you come to think of it, what's the odds? One thing she said is true enough, that poor damn fool of a woman is happy, believing she's got her darling boy back."

Jesse said, "With every expectation of acquiring the hell of a lot of money that doesn't belong to him. A lot of people these days trying to persuade us that there aren't any moral absolutes. The police of all people should know different."

Clock said irritably, "Spare us any quotations from the Torah or Solomon. Will you tell me what the hell we can do about Mr. Smith now?"

"I was already doing a little wondering about the Goodmans. I know it looked so likely that they could be the connection, but one thing that showed up in Allen's report, he's been mailing something to somebody, just the way I suggested, only on a weekly basis."

Clock said, "Love notes to a couple of other cheap blondes."

"I don't think he'd be one to write a note when he could pick up the phone."

"And whatever the hell the truth is, we've lost any last chance to find it out. As Novak says, he'll know now that we're looking into it, and he'll sit tighter than ever. All he has to do. If he was ever tempted to contact a pal from the old days, do a little boasting about the nice soft lay he's on—he won't now."

"I wonder," said Jesse. He drifted back across the room to Mrs. Goodman. She was blowing her nose; she looked up at him with something like hatred. "Mrs. Goodman, you know the other woman—Mrs. Garland—isn't just being jealous, she's afraid her aunt's being victimized by a clever con man. After all, the money was her uncle's. She's got two children of her own—"

She said, "Then she ought to know the feelings in a mother's heart, is all I can say! She ought to know a mother would know her own son! If she hadn't acted so bad to her aunt, called her a fool and some other names, Mrs. Traxler'd let her have some of the money when she dies—but she's got a right to do what she wants with the money, it's her money now. Like she told you that day, if Mrs. Garland wants to apologize to her for those things she said, she'll let bygones be bygones, but I know for a fact Mrs. Garland hasn't been near her, so how's she going to feel? At least she's been happy—I heard her say to him just last night, how it had come to nothing, Mrs. Garland trying to make out he's a crook, because it's not true and there'd never be anything to say it was true, that lawyer couldn't do nothing—and you can't," she said bitterly. "You know you can't. You haven't got a leg to stand on. It grieved her all the more to know how that Mrs. Garland felt, and to think she'd bring the police into it —but they can't do nothing either. There's nothing they can do because there's nothing bad to find out about him—saying he's a crook—a nicer kinder young man I never knew, nice manners and always so cheerful about the house, and Mrs. Traxler looking better and younger than ever I seen her since I come to work for her. She hasn't given any dinner parties or tea parties in a long time, nor she hasn't been going out much except to the bridge club, but that's all going to be different. She's talking about a real big party, some of her old friends, she says she wants to introduce him to lots of people, he'll make new friends and have a whole new life—and she's going to send for some tickets to plays and the grand opera, all the things people like her like to go to—it wouldn't be my idea of how to enjoy myself but that's different, it's the kind of thing that rich people like to do." She was quiet and then said, "They can't do nothing at all. And if she knew—if she knew that woman had brought the police into it, she might have a heart attack and die—I tell you if the police should come to her house, try to ask her questions, or him—she'd just die, and you'd all have that on your consciences. I suppose I should be thankful the police didn't come there to say all these downright insulting things to me, to let her know they were poking around in her private business. She'd die. Can I go now?"

Clock and Novak had come up. Clock said, "We'll take you back to your son's house."

"Am I supposed to thank you? I could take the bus. Calling me names! You can just take your dirty noses out of Mrs. Traxler's personal business—I wouldn't dare tell her what's happened to me today, or him either, they'd be that worried and upset. And what it might do to Mrs. Traxler I don't like to think." She gave her face a final wipe with the handkerchief and stood up. "I was never in a police station in my life before."

"Not when your son's been arrested?" asked Clock.

"That's right, throw it up to me Robert hasn't always been what he should be. I tried to raise him right, but he's weak and he wants nice things for his family. Nobody can say I'm not an honest woman, and whether you believe me or not, I don't tell lies. I never told a lie in my life. Everything I've told you is gospel truth, and nobody can prove any different."

Novak didn't go along; they took her downstairs and drove her back to San Marino Street and let her off and she marched up the broken sidewalk to the house with a straight stiff back. In silence Clock drove up to the nearest main drag, Hoover, and turned right for Hollywood.

Jesse said sadly, "I had a premonition it'd all come to nothing. It was too easy."

"Easy?" said Clock. "It's the only answer, it's got to be, Jesse. That had to be the connection."

"Don't drag your heels, Andrew. Then why didn't he show? As

you said yourself, if he was there, one of Bob Goodman's pals, he'd have shown up. Somebody would have known and said so. This was just another ride on the merry-go-round."

Clock gave a disgusted snort.

"The connection's somewhere else," said Jesse, "if we can ever find it."

"Well, you've eliminated the servants there at the time, at any rate. On account of the picture over the mantel, for God's sake."

"Yes, I should have seen that before, but the connection's somewhere, Andrew, and it's got to be simple. Casual. You know, we haven't taken a look at Mrs. Traxler's friends and acquaintances. So she's thinking of going back to the social life, to introduce her resurrected Tommy to all her old friends. She'll enjoy that, and most of them may be saying and thinking behind her back that she's a gullible old fool, but they won't say it to her face. And he'll put up a good show."

"What about her friends and acquaintances? I don't see any of them—"

"How do we know?" asked Jesse reasonably. "She's been out of the social circle for some time, but she'll have old friends—her bridge club—people they knew before Traxler died, people she's kept up with desultorily. And by this time quite a few of them will probably have grown-up grandchildren. The kind of social circle she'd move in isn't the high-society kind—quiet money, solid money, quiet people, no nightclubbing or crowded cocktail parties. There's been water under the bridge since Traxler died. It's quite possible—we're living in uncertain economic times—that at least a few of those people have suffered what is so delicately called reverses in the last few years. And they—or the grandchildren—could be casting around for ways to replenish the exchequer. It's just possible."

"Oh, don't reach."

"Anything's possible, in a queer situation like this," said Jesse seriously. "One like that could have run across Jerry Smith anywhere, just by chance—a gas station, a bowling alley, a car wash. And got to talking and had the bright idea. Keep an open mind on it. We don't know. And anybody like that would have the necessary information, obviously."

"Talk about up in the air," said Clock. "Well, I suppose it's just possible."

At the Hollywood station he went in the back way, and Jesse tagged after him, having nothing else to do at the moment. Petrovsky was typing a report, and broke off to hear about the session with Mrs. Goodman. He said, "I don't know but what I agree with you, Mr. Falkenstein. She sounds like the genuine dumb article, and when Smith hasn't shown up among Goodman's friends, it looks like another dead end. Oh, Andrew, I'm sorry to tell you we just had a new homicide." Clock growled. "A rape-kill over on Cherokee Avenue. The girl didn't show up at work, so another girl who works in the same office went checking on her on her lunch hour and found her. It was a very messy thing, by what Johnny Mantella says, she was all cut up and obviously raped."

"All we needed," said Clock. "Where's our faithful hound?"

"Gilchrist? He went down to SID to pick the brains of the lab boys. That must be a sort of chancy way to earn a living, writing books. He seems to do all right at it, I gather he's got a nice house in the country, wife and a couple of kids, but it seems to me I'd rather have a regular salary coming in. Oh, that Sergeant from Nevada called back on the redhead."

"That's dead," said Clock.

"As a door nail," agreed Petrovsky. "All they've turned up further—she was mad at the boyfriend, he'd walked out owing her money, and she may have been on the make to pick up a new one."

"So she took a little vacation in L.A. and picked up with the wrong one," said Clock. "What it could look like. I'd better take a look at the homicide."

"Johnny's still over there talking to the other tenants. We turned the lab loose in her apartment. Her name was Laura Goldman, by the way." Clock grunted.

Seeing that they hadn't any time for him, Jesse went back to the Mercedes in the lot and started home. He ruminated about the situation as it looked now, and thought about other places to look for that nebulous connection. He wondered if Charlene Garland would know the names of her aunt's old friends, anything about their families and situations in life. The only one he'd heard about was the fairly anonymous Mrs. Christiansen. He wondered also if Mrs. Goodman's resolve would hold and she'd keep still about being questioned by police. If she was genuine, she was fiercely partisan, and it was possible she might speak privately to Mr. Smith. Or would she?

*　*　*

Monday turned out to be one of the days when he wished he had chosen almost any other profession. He thought he had been making reasonable progress on that divorce settlement, but the other attorney suddenly and unexpectedly dug his heels in and refused the offered terms categorically. His counter offer was nothing short of ridiculous—the complaining wife was fifty-two, in poor health, and the defendant was quite reasonably loaded; and Jesse spent an hour on the phone arguing with his counterpart, and got nowhere.

He had also thought, on that damage suit, that he'd had a very fair chance of getting it settled out of court. It was an unimportant thing, an accidental fall on a heavily waxed floor when the plaintiff was looking at a new house for sale. The attorney for the owner was apologetic when he called just after lunch. He agreed that it wasn't worth the court costs, but the owner was taking a most unreasonable attitude—he claimed that if the damned fool female insisted on wearing three-inch spike heels, she had every reason to fall down anywhere, wax or no wax, and he was damned if he would pay her any damages.

"We wouldn't get it into court for a couple of months," said Jesse, annoyed. "The calendars are full."

"I know, I know, but there it is. I will say, she's asking an unrealistic amount of damages, Falkenstein—"

"And I tried to argue her out of it, but you know women. Vanity, vanity. She says she'll have to have plastic surgery on that knee or she'll never be able to wear a bathing suit again."

"Women," said the other attorney. "Well, I'll talk to my man again if you'll talk to her."

"You know nothing will come of it. Why the hell did I go in for law?"

"It's such a nice refined profession."

He had just hung up the phone when Jean came in and said Mr. Northcott was here, asking if Mr. Falkenstein could see him without an appointment. "I suppose so," said Jesse, repressing a groan. Northcott was the head of the loan department of the local branch of a national bank, a rather colorless, mild-mannered middle-aged man; Jesse had drawn up a will for him, and settled his mother's estate when she had died last year. He stood up to greet Northcott, expecting that he wanted to change his will or possibly change the property deed to joint tenancy, some such little thing, and Northcott came in and told him he was going to be sued for slander by a local politician. "For God's sake!" said Jesse.

"I'm sorry, I know it was a foolish thing to do, I'm afraid I lost my temper—I only attended the rally to ask him about a certain vote in the legislature during the last session, but that man always gets my back up, there's just something about his arrogant attitude—I meant to keep the matter on a dignified level, but the very tone of his voice—I admit it, I called him a thief and a liar, and I do believe he is—"

"You could have voted against him next November," said Jesse.

"There's just something about the man that always riles me," said Northcott.

"Catalytic agents!" said Jesse. "Personal chemistry. Of all the damn fool things to do—"

"Yes, it was," said Northcott humbly.

And where that was going to lead, and what time it would take up—it would be excellent publicity for the politician, who often riled Jesse too, and he wasn't likely to accept a public apology and retreat gracefully.

He spent an hour with Northcott and put off starting the paper work on that until tomorrow. He called the plaintiff in the damage suit and talked to her for another forty minutes without getting anywhere. She was badly scarred for life, she said six times over, the plastic surgery would cost a fortune and wasn't covered by her insurance, and her shoes hadn't one thing to do with the matter, if there hadn't been too much wax on the floor—

Jesse put the phone down and plodded out to the waiting room. It was only five o'clock, but he felt he had put up with enough for one day. He said to his Gordons, "I'm going home. You might as well take off too."

It had been an overcast day, but coming up to the end of the wet season, no unduly unusual weather forecast. But as he turned up Paradise Lane from Coldwater Canyon Drive, the heavens suddenly opened without warning and it began to pour. Southern California had needed rain six months ago, but after a wet winter it was adding insult to injury for a rainstorm to hit in March. By the time he got to the driveway gates it was pouring hard, and he got soaked getting out to open them. Swearing mildly, he braked the Mercedes in the garage beside Nell's, pulled down the overhead door and went in the back way.

Nell, looking completely soaked herself, was rubbing Davy dry with a kitchen towel. "We were way down at the back of the lot," she said crossly, "and it came down in such buckets without any warning—damn, my hair is sopping—"

Davy squirmed and shouted, "All wet!" And Athelstane, who had stopped in the service porch to slurp water from his bowl, ambled in and gave himself a mighty shake, scattering water all over the kitchen floor.

"We'd all better get into dry clothes," said Jesse. "I'll start a fire."

He came down in dry clothes and they had a companionable drink in front of the fire while the rain thundered down on the roof. "I think I'll stick to Dubonnet from now on," said Nell. "It's an interesting sort of taste." Davy scrambled around on the floor with Athelstane patient about being climbed over. Murteza dozed on the mantelpiece. "Just the night," she added, "for baked potatoes and pork chops. I must have had a premonition."

He was still digesting dinner an hour later, when she appeared at the foot of the stairs and said, "I've got to wash my hair. Can you cope with the offspring? Honestly, Jesse—you would read him that one about the bells, he's gone mad about it,

I'm afraid it's going to be another three kittens bit." There had been a period when Davy had incessantly demanded to hear about the three kittens and their mittens, *ad infinitum*. Jesse laughed and got up.

Upstairs in the nursery Davy was bouncing in his crib, clutching the new nursery book. "Bells!" he said to Jesse. "Gay bells? B'ickbats!" He thrust the book at Jesse. "Read about bells!"

Jesse read the old verse obediently, and thought about Judy reading it to Tommy. "Brickbats and tiles,/Say the bells of St. Giles'—Halfpence and farthings,/Say the bells of St. Martin's—Two sticks and an apple,/Say the bells at Whitechapel—"

Hearing about the bells for the fourth time, Davy suddenly drifted off to sleep, and Jesse started downstairs. As he came into the living room the phone rang; he went to answer it in his study.

"Oh, Mr. Falkenstein." It was Charlene Garland. "I had to call you to tell you. Aunt Ruth just called me, and she was quite friendly—I can't get over it—what do you think it could mean?"

"What did she say?"

"Well, she was just a little stiff at first, she said she thought we ought to be on good terms since the family's so small, and she was quite willing to forgive me. She went on to say that she's thinking of giving a few little dinner parties, just quiet ones, for some old friends, and of course she wants to include me. What is behind it?"

"She wants to introduce Tommy into the proper social circle," said Jesse, "and it'll look a lot better if they see you there, tacitly accepting him."

"Oh—of course, I should have seen that. I couldn't. I couldn't sit down at the same table with that man and smile at him and pretend I thought he was Tommy."

"It might be the better part of valor, Mrs. Garland. Keep on her good side." So Mrs. Goodman hadn't said anything; Aunt Ruth was calm and collected.

"I don't know if I could act that well. And it would be hypocritical to let her friends think I do accept him."

"Do you know any of her old friends?"

"Well, by name mostly. There are the Alcorns, they used to be close friends when Uncle Tom was alive, and the Pangborns—Mr. Falkenstein, she talked about getting season tickets to the opera, she hasn't gone to the opera in years! And that series of plays at the Shubert Theater—she said she was going out shopping for evening dresses, and getting her sterling flatware out of the bank—"

"Renewing her youth," said Jesse.

"It's still criminal, I don't care, you can say it's made her happy, but when it's just a delusion—I still want him found out!"

"Well, I'd like to have a talk with you about her friends, if you know much about them, and their families. Maybe you could come to the office for half an hour tomorrow?"

"All right, but I'm afraid I couldn't tell you much, and what have her friends got to do with it?"

"I'll tell you tomorrow."

* * *

That afternoon he was looking over the brief notes he'd taken from the short talk with her—both the Alcorns and Pangborns had families, both men were stockbrokers, and there was another couple named Meyer, and the ladies of the bridge club—when Jimmy came in and said, "There's a Mr. Hamlin here. He says he's from Garrett Associates."

"Oh. Well, show him in."

Hamlin was short and stocky, with wiry red hair and a cheerful round face. "I apologize for disturbing you in office hours, Mr. Falkenstein, but Garrett said to report direct to you, and the more I thought about this one—"

"Sit down," said Jesse. "What've you got?"

"Well, I've been on this Hoffman. The chauffeur. And I think he's mixed up in something very fishy."

"My God!" said Jesse. "Don't tell me, another ride on the merry-go-round!"

8

Hamlin said, "That is a damn soft job he's got, you know. The old lady doesn't go out much, a few times a week, and he hasn't much to do but keep the tank full, change the oil once in a while, keep the Caddy polished up. What I've figured out, he'll check with her every morning—is he going to be wanted or not to take her some place or run an errand, and if he isn't, his time's his own. He's got a little self-contained apartment over the garage, and he eats some of his meals in the kitchen with the housekeeper. But when he goes out on his own, all the time I've been on him, it's just to two places. A big garage down on Vermont, and the public library."

Jesse was interested. "Funny combination."

"You have said it," said Hamlin. "Funny more ways than one, Mr. Falkenstein. That garage, it's called the Acme Body Shop—" Hamlin blew a long stream of smoke and watched it drift upward. "Hah. They seem to do a whale of a big business, quite a few people coming and going, two fellows running the place from what I can see. Hoffman goes there, stays a couple, three hours at a stretch."

"Maybe he owns a piece of it."

"Maybe—and maybe more. It's sandwiched between a big storage warehouse, a Lyons, and a row of little shops—drugstore, stationers', shoe repair. And just the look I've had inside, I think it's fishy."

"Why?"

"A lot of cars in that garage, in a lot out back of the place, a lot of noisy work going on, but nobody seems to come to bring a car in or pick it up. Since I've been watching it. I've sauntered past a dozen times for a look, parked across the street waiting for Hoffman to come out, and I think it's a drop. Hot cars."

"For God's sake," said Jesse.

"It's got that smell. It's a big business now, maybe you know, a big turnover in parts as well as whole cars. The cops could tell you. It's a little different kind of business than it used to be, you get cars stolen to order these days."

"I've heard something about that."

"With the new-car-market slow, there's a big demand for parts. Some of these operations are pretty damned big, connections all over the country, some just small time. But this doesn't look like a legit garage to me."

"I'll be damned," said Jesse.

"I don't know what you want to do about it. I could be wrong, but if I'm right, I suppose we should alert the cops to take a look at it."

"And how Andrew would bless me to hand him something new," said Jesse. "I suppose it ought to be looked at. What do you make of Hoffman aside from that?"

"I've just been shadowing the guy, not delving into his private life. He's about forty, husky, not bad looking. Doesn't seem to have any friends to go to see. Like I say he hits this garage and the public library up on Santa Monica. Takes back an armful of books, comes out with another armful."

"Funny for a chauffeur. A reader."

"Maybe. I went in with him a couple of times, and besides picking out books he spent a while, each time, talking with one of the librarians—the same one. There's a sign on her desk, Alice Stover."

"Even funnier. You're sure about this garage?"

"About eighty percent," said Hamlin. "It smells like a drop to me."

"So I suppose I'd better pass on the tip. I don't know how they'd handle it—"

Hamlin said wisely, "Stake it out. Few people haul cars in for repair at midnight, but that's when the action will be. These people have a little crew of hired hands to rip off the cars to order, it's not the haphazard business it used to be, you know. If it's any kind of big business, there'll be regular orders out for doors, hoods, trunks, engine parts, Chevies to Caddys, all sorts of stuff. But, Mr. Falkenstein, what the hell is one like Hoffman doing mixed up in a thing like that? Why the piddling little job as chauffeur on the side?"

"Not so piddling—you said it's a damned easy job and his living with it. And I suppose it'd be good cover."

"Well, that's so. I'll leave it to you, unless you want us to blow the whistle to the cops."

"I'll take care of it. But I don't know what the hell this could have to do with my business—probably nothing. But thanks. I'll let you know if I want you to carry on with him."

Hamlin said, "If the cops come down and find that is a drop, he won't be there to carry on with. Well, he just went home from the library again, so I don't expect him to go out again today. I'll get back to the office and write you a report."

Jesse sat thinking about that, and presently called the Hollywood station. Clock wasn't in; he talked to Petrovsky. Petrovsky said, "What, another one? We just cleaned out an operation like that a few months back, but they're all over the place these days. Like the man told you, heaps stolen to order for parts, and the parts shipped to hell and gone all over the country. Another part of it, they'll rip off the real oldies to get the VIN number, to add to stolen new cars to make them look legit for resale."

"That's a new twist."

"Not really, it's been going on awhile. Well, this will make a little more work for us. We'll see what comes of it," said Petrovsky. "Thanks for the tip."

Jesse had other work on hand, but he sat there thinking about it some more, and one thing he thought about was that in that type of operation, as Hamlin said, there would be the young fellows hired to rip off the cars. Hoffman and Jerry Smith? Well, a possible tenuous connection, but rather farfetched. He didn't really think that Hoffman could have anything to do with that, but you never knew. He had been devoting some thought as to how to go about having a look at Mrs. Traxler's old friends, and had come to the conclusion that a good rule to follow was the shortest distance between two points. He had names and a few addresses from Charlene Garland, and he looked at the little list wondering where to start. She had said that the Alcorns used to be close friends before Traxler died, and she wasn't sure how closely Aunt Ruth had kept up with them, but Mrs. Alcorn was a member of the bridge club. Possibly the bridge club was a place to start. He sighed, foreseeing a lot of time spent probably for nothing, listening to old ladies talk and talk and nothing useful emerging, but damn it, the connection had to be somewhere. Somehow there had been a contact between Jerry Smith and the source of the information, and it might have been casual, but it should show up with digging. Would it, if it was so casual that it might be buried deep? He felt, on this thing, as if he was grappling with air; nothing solid to get hold of. He sighed again, picked up the phone and dialed the number for Mrs. Christiansen. Charlene had said, a woolly old lady, and over the phone he got what she meant, the soft monotonous voice rippling on and on. "I'm so glad you called me, Mr. Falkenstein. I've been talking to Charlene about this scandalous thing and you've simply got to show Ruth how foolish she's being, really I don't know when I've been more annoyed at her—she's always been headstrong and likes her own way, but at least I always credited her with some common sense. You know, one thing that did occur to me, Mr. Falkenstein, and it is a perfectly dreadful thing to say—or to think—but I had wondered if she's had a little stroke perhaps—the brain damage, you know. I said to Charlene, it might be that she's really not competent in a legal sense, and Charlene said—the dear girl, she's always so forthright—she said we'd never get away with that one, Ruth had all the brains she's ever had, but I really do wonder, Mr. Falkenstein—well, I'd be very pleased to have a talk with you and discuss it at length, her friends must all rally around at a time like this—oh, of course I know the Alcorns, charming people, Marjorie is a dear friend of mine, she's just as upset over this as the rest of us—why, this afternoon would be fine, four o'clock would be fine with me, I'll be very interested to hear what you're doing, Mr. Falkenstein. You know it was I who told Charlene she should consult a lawyer in the first place." He managed to get away from her at last, and looked up the number and called the Alcorn house. They lived in Beverly Hills, and Mrs. Alcorn sounded eminently sensible if a little surprised.

"Oh, Charlene's lawyer. I didn't realize she was taking any steps about it, but I'm glad to know something's being done. My husband and I have been quite worried about it, of course—the whole thing is nonsense, and I could hardly believe it when Ruth told me about it, as if it were possible that this—I don't know what to call him—could be Tommy! Why, I'm sure I don't know how we could help you, but we'd be glad to do whatever we could." He didn't know either. He was probably just woolgathering here, but, he ruminated to himself again, you had to start somewhere, and whatever the source was it had to be someone nominally in contact with Ruth Traxler—then or now. Yes, then or now was the operative point. And where else to look, aside from the servants, but among her friends? He thought suddenly about that cleaning service. Sending people in periodically to polish the floors and windows, wash the walls. The same people? And Mrs. Traxler—the idea slid slowly into his mind, and it was a plausible one, and he liked it. Halfway. Yes, she might talk to her housekeeper, there in the same house; she wouldn't ordinarily be so forthcoming, reminiscing to a casual hired worker just there to do basic cleaning, but that nursery—she wouldn't see one like that sent in there to wash the windows, polish the fire screen, unsupervised; some one of the precious toys might get moved or damaged. She might be right there to see that that didn't happen. And so it might very possibly be, "This was my son Tommy's room, I've always kept it exactly as it was when he was lost to us—no, he didn't die, it was

far worse, he was kidnapped—"and all the rest of it coming
out? The bear Huggy, the rocking horse—he let his mind play
around on that further. What would be the custom for those
people? Would they be given a meal in the kitchen by Mrs.
Goodman? Opportunity for more gossip, more information coming out. Where could he find out about the cleaning service?
And was it worth following up at all? On second thought he
wasn't too sure. He looked back at the list and picked up the
phone again to see if Mrs. Pangborn was home.

* * *

He rather liked the Alcorns. She was a brisk no-nonsense
woman in very smart clothes; he was a taciturn stout little man
with a snub nose and friendly eyes.

"I always thought Ruth had good sense, but maybe most of us
are a little fanatic about one subject, and that was always hers—
since it happened. Tom had tried to tell her at the time, that the
boy was almost certainly dead. I know that body was never
officially identified, but Tom was pretty sure about it himself
and I believe the FBI was too. She wouldn't believe it."

Mrs. Alcorn said in a troubled voice, "I suppose as long as she
felt he could be alive somewhere it eased her grief a little, but it
seemed foolish—refusing to face facts. But when she told me she
believes this man is Tommy come back, I couldn't believe she'd
be so easily taken in—how on earth could he have convinced
her?"

Jesse told them. "She had some reason to be taken in, you can
see, as Mrs. Garland told me. But he could have had that information from—"

"Nearly anywhere!" she said. "The servants. She's always
talked so much about it—and of course it was impossible to tell
her she was being a bore, on a subject like that. But, Mr.
Falkenstein, I would have thought that her lawyers—I know
Tom thought very highly of that firm, he left everything in trust
with them—I should think they'd have been concerned—"

Alcorn grunted in emphatic consent. "When she's handing
over money to this fellow—"

"They seem to take the attitude that it's a waste of time to argue with her. There's no proof one way or the other, you see." He was tired of saying that.

Alcorn said thoughtfully, "I suppose they think even if there was, she'd never accept it or look at it."

"That's about the size of it. And he's putting up a very nice performance."

"It doesn't bear thinking of," she said vigorously. "A common crook taking her for her money—"

"How exactly did you think we might help you?" asked Alcorn.

"Well, can you suggest any possible idea, where he might have got all this information?" They both shook their heads.

"The servants," she said again. "Any servants she's ever had. Did you know that she fired the servants there then, just a few days after the kidnapping? She wasn't rational, of course. Tom was very distressed about it—of course, nobody knew about the kidnapping at the time, you know how everything's kept quiet—"

"Under wraps," said Alcorn, "by the FBI until they know about the ransom, all their investigation going on—there wasn't anything in the papers for ten days or so."

"I remember how surprised I was. I knew there was something wrong, but of course I didn't know what—they were supposed to be coming to dinner that night, and Tom called to say that Ruth was coming down with the flu and they couldn't come —I'd talked to her on the phone just the night before and she was feeling fine, but later, of course—it was an awful time for them both—"

"It killed Tom," he said flatly. "I really believe it did, losing the boy like that. He wasn't so old, you know—younger than I am now." Thomas Traxler would have been older than these people, who would be more likely contemporaries of Ruth. "He was always keen on his business, but he just seemed to lose interest in it all of a sudden after that. Sold out the next year, and just gave up on life. It was a damnable thing to see. But this is a damnable thing too, some plausible crook taking Ruth for all she's got. Don't wonder that Tom's niece is upset about it. Hope you can do something about it, but Ruth's an almighty stubborn woman. If she's made up her mind, you could offer her proof he's the biggest fraud of the century and she'd never look at it."

"That's what Mrs. Garland's afraid of."

"I wish we could think of some way to help you," she said.

On the way home, Jesse decided that this was a waste of time. These people were ordinary nice kind people, at least those he'd seen so far. The Alcorns, in a big house in Beverly Hills, obviously weren't in need of money, and they were genuinely concerned about Ruth Traxler. Mrs. Christiansen, up in the Mt. Olympus Estates, was a plump white-haired pretty old lady surrounded by yards of knitting and portraits of grandchildren, burbling on—Charlene's word for it was a good one—about Ruth having had a little stroke, she couldn't be thinking right or she'd never be acting so foolishly. Of course, the grandchildren —exercising his imagination, he wondered if it was possible that one of the grandchildren was in need of the extra cash, had heard Grandma twaddling on about poor Ruth and her troubles, had run across Jerry Smith and had the bright idea—but that was so far out it wasn't worth thinking about, or was it? What modern grandchild took any notice of what Grandma was talking about, or thought of people Grandma's age still being people, with real-life emotions, loves and hatreds?

When he came in, Nell said, "Andrew's been trying to get you. Are you getting anything at all from the old friends?"

Jesse said wearily, "Nothing but a lot of talk. I think this was another idea that's going to fizzle out." He went into the study and called Clock at home, and Fran answered.

"Just a second, I'll get him. Oh, the baby's fine, and I'm fine too, only poor Andrew's been having all this overtime—the crime rate—"

And Clock said, coming on, "Part of it thanks to you. This damned drop for the stolen cars—"

"Oh, it was, was it? I'll be damned."

"The usual slick little operation, and not so little at that.

Hoffman's brother Earl was running it, but we don't think for very long. Earl was doing time in Susanville up to about eight months ago, on the same charge—he had an operation going over in Monrovia a few years ago. Your Hoffman's got no record at all, and he's claiming loud and clear he hadn't any notion what Earl was up to, he just dropped into the garage to visit his brother. But we're probably going to rope him in—Questioned Documents is working on it now—because he's been keeping the books on the business. Earl was a dropout from school and he's just barely literate. At his other operation, he was working with a fellow named Shepherd who took care of all the paper work. This time he was working alone, and he needed somebody to keep the records." Jesse began to laugh. "It looks as if your man might have been pressured into it, as I say he's got no pedigree, but of course he knew what he was up to. You know something about how that sort of business goes?"

"I've heard this and that."

"Well, it just might be another place to look on the Traxler thing. There'd be a string of young fellows—you can guess the types, some with petty records, and some just louts who don't like to work too hard—hired on a regular basis to rip off the cars to order. And maybe Jerry Smith was one of them."

"I had a stray thought about it, but it's another farfetched one, isn't it?"

"Why?" asked Clock. "Hoffman may not have a record, but he's enough of a crook to be playing in with Earl, pick up the loot wherever it's to be had. He's been living in that house, more or less. That housekeeper will have talked to him. He could very easily have known enough to be the source of the information. He could easily have got talking to Smith, if he was one of the hired hands, and heard about his background. It's a thing to think about."

"Well, I said anything is possible. I suppose it is. I don't seem to be getting anywhere in any other direction."

"We've got him and Earl stashed in jail, but we're keeping the garage open to pick up anybody else who comes drifting in. We got two of the hired hands when we raided the place yesterday, but there'll be more. The way these things go, these boys will be in and out—one of them gets paid off for a job, he may not show up to work again until he runs out of money, and there might have been a dozen or more working for Earl on a week-to-week basis. As we pick them up, we'll be asking them about Jerry Smith, but I thought I'd have a session with Hoffman in the morning, if you'd like to listen in."

"Well, there are things I could be doing at the office, but I'll take you up on that. This is a damned funny development. One thing occurs to me, Mrs. Traxler's going to be annoyed again at Miss McGraw, sending her a crook after the drunk."

"Who's Miss McGraw? Oh, that employment agency. Yes, she'll have to find another chauffeur."

* * *

By the time Hoffman was brought into one of the interrogation rooms at the jail next morning, Questioned Documents had linked him firmly to the business by his handwriting on the books, and Clock told him that to set the ball rolling.

Hamlin had said that Hoffman wasn't bad looking; he was, in fact, just short of being handsome, a big man with lean aquiline features and thick smooth dark hair. He sat at the little table in the tiny interrogation room, in the tan jail uniform, smoking the cigarette Clock had offered him. He'd just compressed his lips at the news and said, "I shouldn't have told Earl I'd help out, is all. I was a damned fool to get mixed up in it."

"Yes, you were, Hoffman."

"And Earl was a damn fool ever to get started on any crooked lay. I tried to tell him, we all tried to tell him—Mother and Dad —he should stay in school and get some sort of education so he could get a decent job, but you couldn't talk to him. He found out he couldn't hold any sort of job, and that's when he went on the crook. I guess how it was, I just got in the habit of helping Earl out when he needed it. And I'm just as glad the folks are both dead, they'd be mad at me for being such a damned fool and getting into trouble with him. Not," he added wryly, "that I was ever so damned ambitious to make a lot of money or be a big shot. The kind of job I had with the Traxler woman suited me fine—I like a quiet life."

"You like to read, don't you?" asked Jesse.

"Yes, I like to read books, why?"

"I just wondered if you'd ever come across a book called *Unsolved Mysteries of the Twentieth Century*, by James Gilchrist."

He shook his head. "I don't think so," he said dully.

"We were just wondering too," said Clock, "if one of the young fellows your brother hired to rip off the cars happened to be a Jerry Smith."

"I couldn't say—I don't remember the name. Who's Jerry Smith?"

"That nice-looking young fellow who's living in Mrs. Traxler's house and pretending to be her dead son, Tommy. Do you know anything about that?"

Hoffman raised his eyes from where he was stabbing out his cigarette in the glass ashtray. He looked surprised and then amused. "Him? Is that his right name? Hell, I heard all about that from that Goodman woman, the housekeeper. How the dear sweet boy's come back from the dead, after the terrible kidnappers hung onto him when he was just a kid, and then left him in an orphanage instead of sending him back to Mama and Papa. And only a stupid pair of females like that could believe such a tale, for God's sake. Of course I knew that young bastard was conning her, who wouldn't? But how she's loving it, and it wasn't anything to do with me, for God's sake. No, I never knew him before, hadn't even heard what his right name was—the old lady calls him Tommy."

"But you'd heard all about the kidnapping, and how she'd kept that nursery just the same."

"I heard about the kidnapping, sure. Not about the rest of all that. I don't recall the Goodman woman ever mentioning anything about all that. I'd only go into the house to have lunch or dinner sometimes. A lot of times I'd fix something for myself in the apartment. The housekeeper never did much talking to me. And I never was upstairs in that house." He was silent, and then said, "Can I ask you something, Sergeant? It sounds kind of stu-

pid, but I've never been in jail before, see. There's—somebody
I'd like to know about this, and I—well I wondered if I could
write a letter."

"Yes, you can write a letter. It'll be read before it's sent out, of
course."

"Oh. Then I guess I won't bother."

"Who would you like to write to?" asked Jesse.

"Just—a friend. A friend. It's a woman at the library, Miss
Stover. She's been nice to me, we've had a lot of interesting
talks. We used to talk about books. She knows a lot about
different kinds of books. But I don't suppose she'd want to hear
from me at that, now this has happened. It doesn't matter."

Outside in the corridor, Clock said, "I suppose we can verify
that, about his never being upstairs. But hell, it says nothing, he
could still have had all the information. Mrs. Goodman's a
talker, don't tell me she didn't come out with all that to him at
one time or another."

"I don't know. I get the distinct impression that Mrs. Goodman doesn't think an awful lot of men, always excepting her
own dear boy and the miraculously resurrected Tommy, for Mrs.
Traxler's sake. She might not have talked much to him."

"Well, we'll continue to follow up the idea, just in case. As we
gather in these louts we'll be asking about Jerry Smith."

"You do that, just in case. No stone unturned. But I don't
think you'll get anywhere. I'd better get back to the office."

But he didn't go back immediately. He drove up to the public
library on Santa Monica Boulevard and found Miss Alice Stover
behind her name sign at a desk labeled Assistant Librarian, and
he told her about Howard Hoffman. She was a rather pretty
woman about thirty-five with a lot of light brown hair and very
bright blue eyes behind big glasses. She said, "Oh, yes, of course
I know him. We've talked quite a lot. He's a very nice man—
mostly self-educated, but a very interesting man really."

"He seemed to want you to know about it," said Jesse.

"Yes. I'm very sorry to hear about it. He's—well, the reason
we got talking, he's a great reader, you see," she said a little ner-

vously. Suddenly she flushed. "I—well, do you think he'd like me to go and see him? Would he be allowed to have—visitors?"

"I don't think he's got many friends, Miss Stover. Yes, you could go to see him."

The flush deepened to bright crimson, and she said bravely, "I will. Thank you for coming to tell me."

Jesse went back to the office to do some work for a change. He didn't think Hoffman had anything to do with Jerry Smith and he was now disenchanted with the idea of any of Mrs. Traxler's old friends having anything to do with Jerry Smith, and he was currently out of ideas where else to look for the connection—that nebulous contact. He talked to the attorney on the other end of the divorce settlement, and made some very slight progress, and presently went out for lunch. He had just got back and was staring at the desk blotter wondering just how to handle Mr. Northcott's little problem, when Jean buzzed him and said, "I've got a Miss Lester on the phone, will you talk to her?"

"Yes, put her through."

"Oh, Mr. Falkenstein," said Mary Lester's crisp businesslike voice, "I've just come across something rather funny, and I thought you'd want to hear about it."

"Oh? Something funny how?"

"Well, you remember that maid—the one working at the Traxler house at the time of the kidnapping—Rose Shaw? All you had on her from the employment agency was her home address at the time, and of course that looked hopeless, it was so long ago. You probably don't remember, it's an address on Larga Avenue in the Atwater area. Well, Mr. Garrett hadn't anything else for me today, and I just thought I'd have a look at it—I'd got interested in this case, you know. It's an old single house, I rang the bell and a woman answered the door and I asked for Rose Shaw—never dreaming anybody there would know anything about her—but she said yes, she was there, she lived there, and I was so surprised I just said, is that the Rose Shaw who once worked for Mrs. Traxler? and she shied back as if—as if I'd held a snake out to her and said, Traxler? Who are you to come mentioning that name here, all her troubles were on account of that Mrs. Traxler, and she slammed the door in my face. And I thought—"

"Now what the hell is this?" said Jesse blankly. "Yes, you thought quite right, Miss Lester. Where are you now?"

"Just up from there, at a drugstore on the corner of Glendale Boulevard."

"All right, you stay there, I'll be with you in half an hour."

* * *

This was an old section of town, with little narrow streets of old houses, very few apartments as yet. The house they wanted was set back from the sidewalk, an old cracker box of a stucco place, long ago painted white with blue trim. Jesse pushed the doorbell, and thirty seconds later the door was opened by a thin elderly woman with wispy white hair, wiping her hands on a wet apron. She looked at Mary Lester and said, "You back again," but any anger had faded out of voice and eyes.

Jesse said, "We're looking for Miss Rose Shaw, Mrs.—"

She said in a dreary voice, "I shouldn't have banged the door in your face, but you upset me, mentioning that name. Shaw, I'm Mrs. Shaw, I'm Rose's mother. What do you want with Rose?"

"I'm an attorney acting for Mrs. Traxler's niece, Mrs. Shaw. I'm afraid it's too complicated a matter to explain in a few minutes, but we'd like to talk to Miss Shaw. Is she here?"

She stepped back and they went in to a small, square, shabby, living room too full of old furniture. She said uneasily, "I don't know if she'll want to talk to you. You're a lawyer? Rose, she couldn't stand up in court about anything."

"It's nothing like that, Mrs. Shaw, we just want to ask her a few questions."

She asked slowly, "Is it about—that family? I don't know if she would answer any questions. I guess I'd better explain about Rose, you coming asking—about her working there." She looked at Mary Lester. "You just caught me by surprise, I've been so worried about her again just lately, and it was all on account of that old business—oh, I ought to ask you to sit down, excuse me." They sat down on a sagging couch. She went on mechanically wiping her hands on the apron. "If it's anything to do with —with courts or the law—I see I got to explain about Rose." She was nervous and ashamed. She sat down on the edge of a chair across the room. "Rose, she was always shy and sort of backward —I don't mean in brains, her brain is good enough—but she never had no confidence in herself, she was always scared she couldn't do things right. She was a couple of years out of high school and she couldn't find a job, well, she was scared half the time to go and ask for one—and it was me said to her, she could be somebody's maid, do housework, she could do that fine, I'd taught her good. And she got that job with the Traxlers, it was the first job she ever had. I never laid eyes on the people myself —she liked it all right, she said Mrs. Traxler was particular and kind of sharp, but she got on all right with her. But all of a sudden she got fired—everybody got fired—it was all on account of their little boy getting kidnapped, and Rose was scared about it, well, who wouldn't be—but when everybody got fired she was scared those police thought she had something to do with it— her and the other ones got fired—there wasn't no other reason they should all get fired. And Rose, she couldn't get over it. She kept expecting she'd be arrested, and I told her not to be silly— but she couldn't get over it, see. It was a long time before she got another job, she was scared to ask, and then when she did she was nervous and kept breaking dishes and such, and she got fired again. And she got it in her head that she'd never be no good at anything—that was the start of it, that Mrs. Traxler firing her for no reason and getting her all worked up—she got it in her head she'd never get another job, and that—that was the start of her trouble."

"What trouble, Mrs. Shaw?" asked Jesse.

She looked more ashamed and nervous; she said reluctantly, "I got to say it. The drink. And—and other things. Oh, you'd hear about it from all the neighbors if I didn't tell you. She'll be all right awhile, but she won't go trying to find a job—and I got to work to support us, I still go out doing housework for people, but it's getting awful hard. And then she'll go off again—I can't be two places at once, always keep an eye on her—she'll go off—on the drink—and—and worse. And she's been arrested for —you know—picking up men. For the money. Oh, I thought I'd never hold my head up again—but you get used to anything, seems like. And somebody's got to try to take care of her. I keep hoping to get her off it."

"I'm sorry, Mrs. Shaw," said Mary Lester gently. "I didn't mean to upset you."

"It was just hearing that name—the start of all her troubles, that was—"

"You got company, Ma?"

They looked up. In the doorway of the hall heading off the dining room was another woman, a thin woman about forty, with untidy dark hair and the raddled remains of yesterday's makeup still showing on her face. Her mouth was slack, her dark eyes too bright. Jesse looked at her, and he thought how many lives had been touched, in different ways, by that brief violent event of one night so long ago. This girl unstable to start with, and using that as an excuse, but—he said, "Rose Shaw?"

"That's me." She came farther into the room; she was wrapped in a soiled and faded pink chenille robe. She raised an unsteady hand to smooth her hair.

And he asked her, "Do you know anybody named Jerry Smith?"

She giggled, and said with an attempt at coyness, "Maybe I do. I might. I know a lot of different fellows."

* * *

When Jesse came in the back door, voices sounded from the living room, and he went down the hall to find Fran and Nell talking animatedly over glasses of Dubonnet.

"Andrew called and said he's doing more overtime, so I invited myself to dinner," said Fran. She was her usual svelte and smart self these days, if slightly plumper here and there. "It's ages since I had a good talk with Nell." Miss Elaine looked her usual serene and beautiful self too, lying dreamily on a blanket on the floor, but when she was hungry she'd let her mother know in no uncertain terms; Fran wouldn't be able to rely on a baby-sitter for some time. Davy, awed to unaccustomed silence by the baby, was watching her fascinatedly.

"And," said Nell, "I think we've been talking to some purpose, Jesse. This funny Traxler thing." She held her Dubonnet up to the light, admiring its tawny color.

"Yes, and something new just turned up on that today, and another very funny thing it is, and I'm wondering if it could possibly mean anything at all. Sometimes the lushes can be—um—disconcertingly cunning."

"Yes, well," said Fran, "you can tell us about the lush in a minute, Jesse, but what occurred to both of us—this Jerry Smith of yours. With the anonymous background at the orphanage. The abandoned child. It's not natural."

"What exactly do you mean by that?"

"Not in this day and age," said Nell, "with all the red tape and record keeping, darling. A hundred years ago, yes, but not now. Everybody's been saying and thinking, this whole business started with Jerry Smith because he hadn't any traceable background, so he could claim to be Tommy Traxler and nobody could prove he wasn't because of that. But, Jesse, an abandoned child gets investigated. The police would have checked into it, tried to find the parents, whoever had been taking care of him. There'd have been records on it with the usual Social Services Department, wherever he was found. And the police wouldn't have handed him over to the Methodist orphanage, for heaven's sake. It would have been Juvenile Hall, and the foster homes."

"And," said Fran, "someone must have found out something. Somebody must have taken some interest in him, and steered him to the Methodist orphanage. Who and how? And what occurred to both of us, suppose the police did find out who he really was, who he belonged to, and the Methodist orphanage knew—they might not have told him."

"Even if it had been foster homes," said Nell, "he might not have known. The impersonality of Social Service departments— but suppose they'd found out he was the illegitimate son of a prostitute or something, the people at the Methodist orphanage might just never have told him, thought it was kinder just to say he'd been abandoned and let it go."

Jesse stared at them.

"Don't you see," said Nell, "it's quite possible there is some record of who he is and where he came from, and if you could find it, well, that would do it, wouldn't it? That would be absolute proof."

Jesse said, "Out of the mouths of babes and sucklings—and me hunting in all the dead ends for the mysterious connection! By God, yes—by God! Why didn't you girls do some detective work on this before?"

9

At least Jesse was interested to have a look at the Methodist orphanage where Jerry Smith had grown up. He had located it without difficulty, on the outskirts of sprawling Long Beach. It was a big square two-story building looking vaguely like a barracks, with a little low-maintenance planting around it to soften the harsh outlines and a small parking lot at one side. It stood in the middle of a short block on the edge of an industrial area, no other building near it. There was one space left in the parking lot; he parked and went up to the front entrance. There was a painted sign over the door; *Methodist Boys' Home* in Gothic letters. He rang the bell. A nice-looking middle-aged woman in a white uniform opened the door to him and he said, "I'd like to see whoever's in charge here."

"Oh, that'll be Mr. Fox, sir. Come in, I'll take you to him." The hall inside was bare and clean and went on ahead into the recesses of the building, with doors on either side. She led him to the first one on the left, opened it and said, "Someone asking for you, Mr. Fox."

The man who stood up from the desk across the room was small and wiry, with a crest of blond hair merging into gray and a thin face, owlish glasses perched on a thin nose. Jesse handed him a card. The room was furnished comfortably if shabbily as a study, with a couple of comfortable chairs, a desk, a tall bookcase, a couple of steel file cabinets. Fox offered him a hand. "Yes, sir, how can I help you?"

"One of my clients is interested in learning the background of one of your boys, Mr. Fox. I'm trying to trace him back, and hope you'll be able to show me some records on it."

Fox looked interested. "Oh, I see. Well, any information I can give you, I'd be happy to help you, Mr. Falkenstein. We don't have a large establishment and, of course, I'd know the background of most of our boys."

"This would be some time back—I believe he'd have come here nearly twenty-one years ago."

Fox's face fell; he looked disconcerted. "Oh, that would be before my time here—I've only been the director here for five years, since Mr. Elliott was forced to retire. His health was beginning to fail—he'd been here nearly thirty years. Records? Well, I'm afraid we don't have the space to keep records on the boys no longer with us, you understand. What was the boy's name?"

"Jerry Smith. I understand the boys leave here at eighteen, he'd have left about eight years ago, by his age now."

"I see. I don't recall the name, of course. Mr. Elliott probably would, he always took great personal interest in the boys when he was the director. We have only around fifty boys on a permanent basis, and we try insofar as possible to take personal interest, make it a real home for them. I'd like you to see our establishment. We don't have a large endowment, but we're proud of what we've been able to accomplish. Of course quite a few of the boys are only with us on a temporary basis—there'll be family circumstances, illness and so on, and we keep them until it's possible for them to return to their families. But then again we do have the genuine orphans whose parents were church members or who are referred to us from some other source, who spend their formative years with us."

"This boy was an abandoned child, and I don't know how he came to be here."

"Oh, really," said Fox, surprised. "Now that is most unusual, but as I say I wouldn't remember about it. I wonder if Mrs. Patterson might remember him, she's our matron and has been here

nearly fifteen years. You see, we have a rather spartan routine
here. We have two good women as cooks in the kitchen, and a
very capable janitor who looks after our furnace and does all the
many odd jobs, and we have found it excellent training for the
boys to keep up the various daily tasks of cleaning the dormitories—we haven't a large staff. Fortunately, we've been able to
qualify under a state grant for medical aid to private organizations, the boys have regular checkups. I think we just might
ask Mrs. Patterson, if you'll come with me." He led Jesse out to
the hall again and up a steep flight of uncarpeted stairs to an
upper hall. As they went he chatted on, paused to open a door
to the right. "One of our dormitories—you can see we try to provide each boy with as much comfort and privacy as possible."
Jesse duly admired the big hygienic room with the rows of single beds, each with a locker and bed table, tall windows. "So far
as possible we group the boys by age, and we appoint the older
boys to keep order, it all works out quite well—the matron helps
to oversee the younger ones, of course, but we don't take boys
under five. Of course we have to have some strict regulations,
it's necessary as you can imagine—the boys attend the local public schools, and they often join extracurricular activities, but
they're always required to be in by six when our evening meal is
served. They always attend church services each Sunday—our
church has a bus—and the smaller ones attend Sunday school."

It all looked clean and bright, if not very homelike, thought
Jesse. At the end of the hall Fox tapped at a door, poked his
head in and said, "Oh, Mrs. Patterson, I hope I'm not disturbing you."

"Not at all, haven't got any patients in at the moment, and I've
got the little ones settled down at finger painting in the dining
room. We've had quite a lucky winter, only that one outbreak of
flu." She was a large motherly-looking woman. This tiny cubicle
was a cross between office and supply room, with shelves holding a miscellany of bottles and jars, a small desk, an old rocking
chair. An open door gave a glimpse of another small dormitory,
evidently the infirmary.

"Mrs. Patterson, Mr. Falkenstein here is inquiring about a boy who would have left us about eight years back, a Jerry Smith. Do you remember anything about him?"

She ruminated and said, "Allergies. I do remember him vaguely, he was one of those with allergies. He had to have special injections now and then."

"Do you remember anything about how he came to us?"

"Oh, I wouldn't know anything about that, Mr. Fox. That would have been arranged with Mr. Elliott and the board of sponsors."

"Yes, of course. You see," he said to Jesse, "we have a limited capacity. When a boy is referred to us and we have room for him we will accept him, of course, but the decision is up to our director and the board of sponsors."

"I seem to remember," said Mrs. Patterson, "that he was a nice boy, very polite."

"Well, thank you," said Fox. "I wonder now—I'm afraid none of the rest of the staff could help with the matter, Mr. Falkenstein," as they went back down the hall. "The other women are nearly always busy in the kitchen, they haven't much to do with the boys. I'm always available, if they have any little problems at school or otherwise, to offer advice—and we do try to give them as much personal attention as possible—and people are really very good, one of the teachers at the local high school comes once a week as a volunteer to teach the older boys woodworking, we have quite a well-equipped craft room in the basement—and a men's group at our church sponsors regular trips to sports activities and so on. But as I explained to you, I've only been here since Mr. Elliott retired, and when a boy leaves us we really have no space to continue keeping his records. Of course while a boy is here, regular school and medical records are kept—"

"Could I talk to this Mr. Elliott?" asked Jesse. "Where would I find him?"

"Oh, yes, of course, I was about to suggest that. He is living with his sister, I have the address, of course. He and his wife were the mainstay of our home for over thirty years—Mrs. Elliott acted as matron—and having no family of their own they really regarded the boys as their family, such fine people, such good people. It was a sad loss to Mr. Elliott when she died so suddenly—Mrs. Patterson is very good and kind, of course, but it must have made a great difference to him the last few years he was here."

"Yes, I'm sure it did."

Back in his study Fox opened a drawer and consulted an address book. "His sister is a widow, you see, and as he had made this his home for so many years and had no other, it seemed sensible for him to go to her. I will just write the address for you. I haven't seen Mr. Elliott for some time—I'm afraid his health is failing even more these days. But his mind is still quite active, and I'm sure he'll be able to help you in some way, Mr. Falkenstein—may I just ask why your client is anxious to trace the boy's background? I don't believe we've ever had a similar inquiry."

Jesse said vaguely, "Well, it may be a matter of a legacy." He reflected with wry humor that that was all too true.

"Oh, I see, how very interesting. Well, I hope Mr. Elliott can be of some help to you."

It was an address in Santa Ana. Jesse wasn't familiar with Orange County and had quite a hunt for the place; it was a big town. He stopped to ask directions, and finally found the house —an old California bungalow on a wide street of older homes. He left the Mercedes at the curb, went up and rang the bell, and a stout pleasant-faced woman opened the door to him. "I'd like to see Mr. Elliott if he's feeling well enough. Mr. Fox suggested I should see him—it's something to do with the boys' home."

"Oh, yes, I'm sure he'd be glad to talk to anyone, the days go pretty slow for him. Come right in." It was a long combination living-dining room, typical of these old bungalows. "Ed, here's someone Mr. Fox sent. He wants to see you about the home."

Elliott was sitting in an armchair at the living end of the room; he was a thin frail-looking old man with a little halo of white hair, a gentle much-lined face, faded blue eyes. He was dressed neatly in old slacks and an open-necked shirt, and had been reading a fat book laid open on his lap. Jesse introduced himself and said, "It's a matter of tracing one of the boys who was at the home, Mr. Elliott. One of my clients is concerned to find out about his background, and as it was some time back Mr. Fox thought you might remember."

Elliott offered a cordial, slightly shaking hand. "Of course, any way I can be of help to you, sir. Sit down and tell me what you want to know. My poor old body may be tired out these days, but by the grace of God I seem to have kept my mind intact, and my memory is quite good, I flatter myself. Do sit down. Now, what was it?"

Jesse sat down in a hard little rocker across from him and said, "A boy named Jerry Smith, Mr. Elliott. I understand he was found abandoned. Do you remember anything about him?"

Elliott's expression quickened with interest. "Dear me," he said. "Jerry Smith. Indeed I do remember, Mr. Falkenstein, because of the circumstances. In my time we had a great many boys pass through the home, and while we tried to give them all some personal attention, naturally there were always a few who stood out from the rest, for one reason or another—not always a positive reason, I'm afraid. In any crowd of boys there'll be the occasional obstreperous one, but also there were those with exceptional scholastic ability or some other talent. But as perhaps Mr. Fox explained to you, the great majority of our boys come to us from quite respectable and, well, known backgrounds. Sometimes we would have a boy for only a year or two, until a parent was able to take him again—straitened circumstances, illness— and quite a few of the boys had some relative—a grandparent, an uncle—who came to visit, gave them some sense of belonging to a family. To my recollection, the boy you mention is the only one we ever had where nothing at all was known of his background. May I ask what your client's interest is?"

"It may be a matter of a legacy, if we could trace him back at all. How did he come to be in your home, Mr. Elliott?"

Elliott took off his glasses and began to polish them on his handkerchief. "I don't see," he said regretfully, "how you could ever trace where he came from, Mr. Falkenstein. It was a very strange circumstance, very strange. In the ordinary way the poor youngster would have been taken in charge by the authorities, but as it happened we had a vacancy at the home at the time, and Mr. Hardy felt very strongly that we should take him—he made a special appeal to our board of sponsors. You see, Mr. Falkenstein, while the home was endowed many years ago, as money has lost its value our appropriations have naturally dwindled, and we make it a practice to charge a very nominal fee for the boys whose relatives can in any way afford to contribute to their support. Of course, in cases of genuine need this is waived, and at any given time roughly half of our boys are supported entirely by the home. In this particular case, there was of course no question of a fee being paid. Another consideration was that our boys usually come from Methodist families, at least good Christian families, and there was some objection raised by one of the sponsors to taking in an unknown boy. But Mr. Hardy put it to them very strongly that we have a Christian duty to care for the stranger and the oppressed, and of course he was quite right, quite right. There is the object lesson of the Good Samaritan." Having polished his glasses to his satisfaction, Mr. Elliott put them back on and looked at Jesse severely.

"But what did this Mr. Hardy have to do with it?"

"Oh, dear me, I fear I'm explaining this very badly, Mr. Falkenstein. Mr. Hardy was the one who brought the boy to us —the Reverend Mr. Hardy, he was and in fact still is the minister of a church in Santa Monica. And I'm afraid he was put to a great deal of trouble in the matter, as indeed we all were. There is no one who respects law and order more than I do, sir, but there are occasions when the law and its representatives can be foolishly arbitrary and difficult. It wasn't only Mr. Hardy who was forced to argue with authority, I came in for my share of responsibility too. It was all very trying, very trying indeed."

"But what exactly were the circumstances?" asked Jesse patiently.

"Oh, haven't I explained that? I beg your pardon. You see, Mr. Hardy was brought into the matter when one of his parishioners took the boy to him, not knowing what else to do. The boy had

been abandoned by the people who had been caring for him—
and not, it emerged, caring for him at all well—evidently not the
parents, by what the little boy could tell us—he was quite
young, you know, only five or six. And they were strangers to
this church member and his wife, they had I believe lived next
door to them for only a brief period. Mr. Hardy was a bachelor
at the time and at a loss to know what to do with the boy, so he
brought him to us temporarily. But of course the authorities had
to be informed, and I understand that they made every effort to
trace the people who had abandoned the boy, with no success at
all. It was then we began to have trouble with them—the authorities, that is. The police all but demanded that we hand the
child over, to be taken to their Juvenile Hall, and there was a
perfectly terrible woman from one of the Social Services departments who was quite insistent on taking charge of him—I really
don't know how I would have dealt with her if it hadn't been for
my dear wife—Mabel had the courage of a lion, and she faced
up to the woman like a real heroine, asking her if she really
believed the child would be better off in a series of foster homes
than receiving a good Christian raising with us. And Mr. Hardy
was still arguing with the board of sponsors at that time."

"I see," said Jesse. "The police never traced the people who
had abandoned him at all?"

"No, they were never able to. I believe they reached the conclusion that the people had been using a false name. Obviously,
if they had ever been able to locate any relatives, we would
have heard about it, and we never did. As I say, Mr. Hardy
finally persuaded the sponsors to agree, and we kept the boy
permanently. He was with us until he was eighteen, and he
turned out to be quite a satisfactory boy. Not outstanding in any
way, but a quiet, good boy."

"But couldn't he tell anything about his parents, his family? A
boy of five or six—"

"Very little. All he could say was that he'd been living with
some people he knew as Uncle Bernie and Aunt Mae—and there
might have been some reason for that," said Elliott, looking suddenly angry. "We had him checked over physically, of course,

and the doctor said there was evidence of gross malnutrition. And the boy himself volunteered that the woman used to give him pills which made him sleepy. Inexcusable!" said Elliott. "The things people will do to children! The boy was much better off with us, and certainly he had a better bringing up than he would have had in those foster homes. But you can see that there's no possibility of finding out exactly what his background was."

"Yes, I see. Do you know where the boy went when he left you?"

"Ah, there I'm afraid I fail you. Of course we don't, we can't, arbitrarily dismiss boys from the home when they turn eighteen, but they are all aware that they'll be expected to stand on their own feet and look after themselves. Sometimes the counselors at the high school are of help. But as soon as they find jobs, they leave us to support themselves. Let me see, the Smith boy must have left us at least eight or nine years ago, and I'm afraid I don't recall what sort of job he went to."

"This Mr. Hardy, that was all he knew about the child?"

"I believe so. You could talk to him if you like, as I say he's still the minister of that same church. I could give you the address, or it would be in the phone book. But I doubt very much that you could find out anything more about the boy, Mr. Falkenstein."

Jesse got up. "Well, thanks very much, sir."

* * *

If he was going to see the police, he had to go to Santa Monica anyway, and it was just getting on for noon. He stopped at an anonymous coffee shop for a sandwich and found the right Methodist Church in the phone book.

The Reverend Mr. Hardy was there, but told him he was lucky to catch him, he had only dropped by the church to look up some parish records. He was a middle-aged man with a thin ascetic face. He told Jesse all over again what Mr. Elliott told him about Jerry Smith. "I was much younger then and it shocked me—it shocked me dreadfully—the irresponsibility and cruelty—but there are too many people like that in the world. No, the authorities never discovered anything more about it. They were terribly difficult to deal with, they kept badgering the Ropers unmercifully, and of course they didn't know a thing about it."

"The Ropers?"

"Yes, the people who brought the boy to me," said Hardy. "They were members of the church—in fact, Mr. Roper still is, his wife died several years ago. He lives just around the corner from the church, if you'd like to talk to him. But why anyone should be interested in that boy after all these years—I'm afraid there's no question of finding out anything more now."

* * *

Benjamin Roper was a paunchy bald old man with a reedy voice. He lived in a shabby two-room apartment in an old building on an old street, and he welcomed Jesse in and listened to him with interest. He sat and rocked back and forth in an old-fashioned platform rocker, with a fat calico cat on his lap, and he stroked the cat mechanically. He said to Jesse, "Excuse it if that chair isn't just so comfortable. I only need enough for myself. My son pesters me to come and live with them, but it wouldn't do—the grandchildren racketing around, and that blasted TV on half the time, and I like to go to bed early. Yes, sir, that was one of the queerest things ever happened to us. I'd be glad to tell you about it, you being interested. I remember it like it was yesterday. See, Joyce and me, we'd just moved into that apartment, it was over on Arizona Street. Harry, that's our son, he'd just got married and we didn't need such a big apartment no more, so we'd moved. I was working for the Santa Monica Bus Company, over thirty years I worked for them. And we'd been there maybe a couple of months when these people moved into the next apartment. They said their name was Hughes, but I guess the police decided later on it wasn't at all. They'd just said that. I always thought myself they came there with the idea of getting rid of that poor little kid, just walking off and leaving him. Acourse I was out all day, but Joyce always tried to be neighborly with people, she took some cake or something next door and tried to get to know the woman, but she said she wasn't friendly at all. Joyce felt sorry for the little boy, she said he looked kind of peaked. The only thing the woman told her was that he was her sister's kid, and the sister was having some kind of trouble with her husband and they were keeping the kid just for a while. They was only there about a week, when one Sunday morning we was just leaving for church, and there's the door of the next apartment open and the kid standing there, just with some dirty ragged old clothes on. And he says, 'Please,' he says, 'I'm awful hungry, could you please give me somethin' to eat?' he says. He says, 'They've gone away somewhere,' he says. Well, you can imagine we was sort of took aback, but Joyce, she thought about the kid before anything else, and she took him back to our place and give him some kind of cereal or eggs or whatever, and he ate like a young wolf. All dirty he was, like he hadn't had a bath in a month, or I guess a solid meal either. Well, we talked it over, and we went next door and looked, and they were gone all right—no clothes or nothing left, the refrigerator cleaned out. Well, that was a facer, as they say. We didn't hardly know what to do, but call the police, and that poor little kid—a cute blond kid he was about five, real towhead, and you know he said, 'Thank you,' after he'd gobbled down what Joyce gave him—somebody had taught him real polite manners, whatever kind of folks he came from—it didn't seem right to hand him over to the cops. But Joyce said we should ask the minister, he'd know the right thing to do, so that's what we did. And we like to never saw the last of those cops, the minister had to call them, naturally, and they kept coming back and pestering us, didn't we know any more about the Hugheses, and the manageress of the place too, but all she could say that they'd paid the first and last month's rent and she didn't know where he worked or anything. And the only thing Joyce and I could tell them, the only thing that woman had said to her at all, was that Hughes, he was some kind of a representative for a union somewhere."

The cat woke up suddenly and jumped off his lap and Jesse felt as if he'd seen a ghost.

* * *

"My God, don't you see it?" he said to Clock and Gilchrist. "My God, that could damn well be Tommy Traxler! He really could be Jerry Smith."

"The union," said Clock. "A vague connection, but, Jesse—"

Gilchrist asked acutely, "Just when did all this happen?"

"I got a date out of Roper—it was the January after the kidnapping in September." He was pacing up and down the living room while Nell listened silently with the other two. Davy was napping upstairs, this quiet Sunday afternoon. "Don't you see it? Kendall said that in the average case of kidnapping if the child gets killed it's accidental. Suppose the Traxler boy wasn't killed. Even suppose the Carnahans meant to keep him themselves until they picked up the ransom. As soon as they knew the FBI was sniffing around—and that was damned soon—they'd find a place to hide him better. I don't think they would have kept him, it'd be too dangerous. They had some place to stash him while the heat was on, and where better than with one of those union members who thought the Carnahans were new Saviors to lead the masses out of slavery? Somebody who would've done anything for the Carnahans?"

"And why didn't they return him to the Traxlers once the ransom got paid?" asked Clock.

"Have you ever thought how difficult that might be, Andrew? With the Feds keeping an eye out? That's the second reason the snatched child gets killed, especially one old enough to notice things and talk. Very possibly—if this could be so—the people who abandoned him weren't the ones who'd had him all along—maybe he was moved around with different people, the Carnahans would have had pals among union members all over the place. By then the story of the kidnapping was out—"

"Exactly," said Nell. "It's your story, but how many people do you think would be willing to risk that charge just to oblige the Carnahans?"

Jesse made an impatient gesture. "So it was just the one couple. And then the heat was on, and just how the hell were they going to send him back? I can see everybody getting cold feet on it. Piece it together! If that was the Traxler boy, they'd been keeping him under wraps as well as they could—the sleeping pills, so he wouldn't make any noise or call attention to himself. Yes, those sleeping pills, and all the rest of it—that wouldn't have done his mind any good, would it? And a child's mind could work in some queer ways, you know. Four and a half months would be eternity to a child of that age—"

"Would they have really kept him that long, Jesse?" asked Nell, wrinkling her brow.

"If that was the Traxler boy, I think they got stuck with him," said Jesse. "Look, they were all crooks and damned insensitive, but they weren't monsters, Nell. Nobody was planning to murder him and get left with a body to get rid of. It could just have gone on, nobody knowing just what to do about it, until the people who had him got fed up and slid out from under the easiest way. They were probably damned scared by then, too. And another thing—the way a child's mind works—he might have accepted quite readily that his name was Jerry Smith while he was with them and something different at home. Home!" said Jesse angrily. "They may have hoped he'd be identified, or they may not have cared—and by then, for God's sake, the kidnapping had died out of the press, and when the boy hadn't shown up the Feds and Traxler himself were sure he was dead—and the Santa Monica police treated it as just another case of abandonment! How much might he remember of home, and Mama and Papa, and Judy and all the toys, after that long of being fed the sleeping pills? All that sifting down into his unconscious mind—"

"By God," said Gilchrist softly, "it'd be an ironic thing if that could be true, Falkenstein. It just might be true."

"I think I'd like a doctor's opinion on that," said Clock dubiously.

"It damn well could be!" said Jesse savagely. "The dates, the circumstances. The cute little blond boy with the polite manners. And if it is so, Jerry Smith's been telling a gospel true story all along, everything he said is so. All those queer bits and pieces at the bottom of his unconscious mind—"

"Triggered off," said Gilchrist, "by my slick little account of that snatch, and the photograph of the Traxler house."

"That's right—that's right. It's just the kind of thing that might have triggered off his memory after all those years."

"You're just using your imagination overtime," said Clock. "There's still absolutely no proof one way or the other. I will say, none of the hired hands we picked up at that hot-car drop ever seemed to have heard of a Jerry Smith. But you've got nothing at all to say this latest wild idea is true. And so far as I can see you never will have anything to say yes or no. My God, that'd be a queer thing if he really was the Traxler boy—everybody putting him down automatically as a con man."

Jesse barked a laugh. "Except Ruth Traxler, and a mother would know her own boy! Ironic is the word."

"But there's no way to know for certain," said Nell.

Gilchrist lit a new cigarette and leaned back. "There's one way to find out if Tommy Traxler's dead or alive," he said dreamily. "I'll agree with you, Falkenstein, I don't think anybody murdered him later. If Tommy Traxler is dead, he died by accident the night he was snatched. And the only people who could say yes or no on that are the Carnahans."

They all stared at him.

◦ ◦ ◦

Charlene Garland had listened to him quietly, her grave eyes fixed on his face. As he might have expected, her modest house in West Hollywood was well kept, this comfortable living room tidy and well furnished. The boy and girl were somewhere at the back of the house.

"I'm sorry to have to tell you all this, and of course it's still nothing, it says nothing one way or the other. No, I didn't go to see the police—they may not have kept records on it this long, and in any case, when the boys' home never heard any more about it, it's obvious that the police never came up with any lead to the so-called Hughes couple."

She drew an unsteady breath. "Do you really think that could have been Tommy? That—that—he *is* Tommy?"

Jesse spread his hands. "It's possible," he said helplessly. "It's just possible, Mrs. Garland."

She said, "If that could be true—if he really is, and everything he said is true—and Aunt Ruth right all along—it's an awful thought that nobody's—nobody's welcomed him, or been glad to see him. But we don't know. There's still no proof."

"I'm beginning to think we never will know," said Jesse morosely.

"Well," she said practically, "if there's no way to stop Aunt Ruth believing him, at least I'm glad to know there is this possibility—that he's honest. I can't feel it's so, but all that—Mr. Falkenstein, what do you really think?"

"I don't know," said Jesse. "I don't know what to think and whatever's true—that's God's truth."

10

"This is a waste of time," said Jesse as he turned onto Chandler Boulevard.

Gilchrist sat back in the passenger's seat of the Mercedes and blew smoke calmly. "Not at all, it may tell us right away what we want to know."

"You don't suppose for a second, even if we can locate the Carnahans, they're going to open up and say, we cannot tell a lie, it was us? The statute of limitations doesn't run out on kidnapping. They probably knew the Feds suspected them at the time, and that they were damned lucky to get away with it."

Gilchrist said, "Exactly. They've been congratulating themselves that they got away with it all these years. I don't expect them to come apart and admit it, no, all I say is that—after all these years—there's bound to be some reaction if we face them with it. Some reaction that we can evaluate psychologically, if it's only a facial expression, an involuntary exclamation—"

"To hold up in a court of law, for God's sake?"

"It doesn't have to hold up in court, Falkenstein. All we want to know is the bare fact, was the boy killed or did he survive the snatch? If we can get some definite answer on that, we'll be that much further ahead, at least we'd know whether Jerry Smith is an imposter or not."

Jesse grumbled, "I still think it's a wild idea. And where is this damned place?"

"Just up ahead—I can see the sign."

The manufacturing plant once owned by Thomas Traxler covered a couple of acres, this far out in the San Fernando Valley. There were two long low buildings, a large parking lot at each side. The sign across the top of the front building read, KRAFT-EWING PRECISION PRODUCTS, A DIVISION OF NORAMCO, INC. Jesse found a slot in the parking lot and they walked up to the front entrance where a little planting of dwarf palms enhanced plate-glass windows and door. Inside, there was a small anteroom with a counter across it, behind a switchboard where several girls sat, and four doors at one side labeled with names. A row of windows behind the switchboard gave a view of the parking lot, this building evidently divided into two wings. A sleek blond girl at a desk behind the counter said, "Can I help you?"

"We'd like to see your personnel manager," said Gilchrist.

"If it's about a job, our quota—"

"Nothing like that, we want some information about a couple of former employees."

"Well, I don't know, some of our work is classified, I can see if Mr. Safford is free. If you'd have a seat—"

There was a low padded bench built against one wall. They sat down and Jesse stretched out his long legs and contemplated them gloomily. "So you fancy yourself as a psychologist."

"You learn one hell of a lot about people, working for a newspaper," said Gilchrist. "This may be a little gamble, but we may as well take it."

Ten minutes later the blonde put down her phone, said, "Mr. Safford can give you a few minutes, if I could have your names?"

Jesse gave her a card. She came through a flap in the counter and led them to one of the doors at the side of the room, labeled *Rodney Safford,* preceded them through it to lay the card on the desk. It was a small office with filing cabinets shoulder-high on three sides, a view from the window over the parking lot with its sea of cars. Safford was a spare colorless man with sandy hair, the jacket of his suit draped over the back of his desk chair. He regarded Jesse's card and said, "Well, what can I do for you? Sandra said some information about some of our employees?"

"Former employees, I think," said Gilchrist. "Frank and Pat Carnahan."

Safford's expression sharpened and his brows rose. "Oh, and just what's a lawyer's interest?"

"We think they may have some information we're after," said Jesse. "Do they still work here?"

Safford said dryly, "Not for a while. But yes, I know the name."

"We don't know the men personally," said Gilchrist. "Just, you might say, their reputation."

Safford said even more dryly, "I see. And they may have information you want. Well, I can tell you something. They were both working here when the plant changed ownership twenty years ago—"

"When Thomas Traxler sold out," said Jesse.

"Oh, you know that? Yes. I came in as personnel manager at that time. The Carnahans—" Safford sat back in his desk chair and poked a ball-point pen at the desk blotter thoughtfully. "You know they were very active in the union movement?"

"Yes, we know that," said Jesse. "Not to say violently active, if that's the word."

Safford laughed shortly. "Sometimes I wonder if this whole-sale education does any good at all," he said unexpectedly. "The average man doesn't seem able to use reason in the abstract sense. The men like the Carnahans—of course, the idea that capital and labor are natural enemies is pure Marxist theory, and it makes about as much sense as the rest of it. The fact is, they're two sides of the same coin, they can't get along without each other. It makes better sense to say that the capital and labor of Company A are natural enemies of the capital and labor of Company B, in competition. You'd think anybody who can add two and two would see that, but men will let prejudice rule—and men like the Carnahans just keep the pot boiling, egging them on, aware of what they're doing. Whether any of them admit it or realize it, they're after power as much as any would-be dictator." He sat back in his chair and ruffled his sandy hair. "Sorry. End of lecture. Yes, they were both here when I came in, but Pat Carnahan left a couple of years later. He went on into a slightly higher echelon of union representation, got a job somewhere back East with the national union. He was killed during an outbreak of violence in a strike against a steel mill about fifteen years ago, I think."

"Oh," said Jesse.

"What about his brother?" asked Gilchrist.

"Frank Carnahan was still working in our machine shop up to a couple of years ago, when he had to take early retirement, some health problem. I wouldn't know where he is now, presumably still somewhere in the area."

"Well, that's that," said Gilchrist. "I suppose we can look in the phone book."

"Be my guest." Safford produced a local book. "I seem to remember it was an address in Burbank."

They looked and found him listed on Catalina Street in Burbank. "Thanks very much," said Jesse.

"Not at all—hope you get whatever you're after."

They went out to the parking lot and started back for Burbank, and Jesse said, "A waste of time."

"We don't know until we look."

The house on Catalina Street was an old stucco place on a street of pleasant well-maintained homes. There was a woman in the front yard next door pruning some rose bushes in a bed by the porch. She watched them up the front walk. Jesse pushed the doorbell four times, but there was no response. They started down the walk again. The woman came over to the driveway between the houses and asked, "You're looking for Mr. Carnahan?"

"That's right," said Jesse.

"He's in the hospital. He's pretty bad, I hear. He's got cancer and they don't expect him to live very long. You friends of his?"

"No, we just want to see him on business."

She shook her head. "Well, you could see him in the hospital, I guess. I don't know what'll happen to the house, I'm sure. They never had any children and his wife died a couple of years ago. I don't think there's any family at all. It's St. Joseph's Hospital here in town."

In the Mercedes, Gilchrist said, "It's still worth a try. Maybe even more so now."

It was a big sprawling pile of a place with a generous parking lot. They went into the lobby and up to the desk, and Jesse asked where they could find Mr. Frank Carnahan. The white-uniformed woman at the counter said, "Visiting hours don't start until two, sir, but I'll get you the room number." When she came back she said, "That'll be all right, you can go up. It's three-four-teen."

They rode up in a smooth elevator and Gilchrist said, "Wonder why we're privileged?"

On the third floor a maze of doors opened out before them, and they passed two cross-corridors before coming to a nurses' station. There was a young intern standing at the desk, and he turned when he heard Jesse's question to one of the nurses, and came out to them. He was a tall lanky dark fellow with sharp features. "Carnahan?" he said. Jesse absentmindedly handed him a card.

"Yes, I understand we're outside visiting hours but the receptionist downstairs said—"

"Yes, that's all right. Patients in this wing are privileged, you could say," and he gave them a one-sided smile. "All on borrowed time. You wouldn't be family members?"

"No, we want to see him on a matter of business."

"Oh," said the intern. "The reason I asked, he's never had any visitors at all, and that can make a difference to a patient's morale, you know. You can talk to him, but he's pretty weak."

"How long has he got?" asked Jesse bluntly.

The intern shrugged. "Anybody's guess. He's riddled with cancer. But the last week or so he's been relatively free of pain, he's not much doped up."

A nurse led them halfway down the corridor to a two-bed

room, indicated the bed by the window. The curtains were drawn between the beds, and the man in the nearest bed looked to be comatose, breathing quietly. Frank Carnahan lay on his back in the other bed, the sheet drawn up on his chest. He had been a big man, but his frame was wasted, his face thin and drawn, his skin gray under a gray stubble of beard. He opened his eyes and looked up at them. "Who the hell are you?" he asked in a faint husky voice.

"Nemesis," said Gilchrist. "All we want to know, Carnahan, is what happened to Tommy Traxler? Did he die that night?"

Carnahan's expression never changed. Jesse said, "I'm a lawyer, Carnahan. The law can't touch you now, and it's a long time ago. The FBI was pretty sure at the time that it was you and Pat who snatched the Traxler boy. It was, wasn't it? You could do some good now and right a few wrongs, if you tell us the truth —did the boy die that night?"

Carnahan opened his mouth and said distinctly, "Go to hell."

Gilchrist said brutally, "You're dying, Carnahan, and you might do one good thing before you pass out, to even the score and make it a little better for you on the other side."

Carnahan's thin mouth stretched in a mirthless grin. He said faintly, "That's a lotta bullshit. You die—you go out—like a light."

"Listen, Carnahan," said Jesse. "The Feds always thought you had the boy, and that he died by accident that night—that was the body found six months later. Was that so? All we want is a yes or no."

Carnahan met his eyes and gave him a wolfish grin. He said, "Go—to—hell," and he shut his eyes and turned his face to the wall.

* * *

Jesse was back in his office, having just seen a client out, when Gil Allen called at four o'clock. "Thought you'd like to know your boy's just formally joined the Beverly Hills Country Club. He spent a while in the manager's office, and the manager came out with him and shook hands and welcomed him as a new member. He'll probably sign up for a course of golf lessons next."

"Am I supposed to say three cheers?" asked Jesse.

"Well, he seems to be settling down to the life of a young gentleman. I'll bet Mrs. Traxler's pleased. There was a caterer's truck in the drive this morning—suppose she's planning a blow-out of some kind?"

"Probably," said Jesse gloomily.

"Do I carry on with him? He's not leading us anywhere and I doubt if he ever will. If he's got old pals around, the way you thought, he's turned his back on them now he's moving in higher social circles."

Jesse said again, "Probably. I think we'll call it a day, I'll let Garrett know definitely by tomorrow." He couldn't go on wasting Charlene Garland's money for nothing. Presently he went home; at least the weather was settling down to a warm spring, and rain was over until fall. He and Nell had a companionable drink before dinner, and after dinner he read to Davy, inevitably ending up with the *Bells of London Town*. He would call Garrett in the morning and call off the private eyes. This whole sorry business was winding down to an ignominious finish, fizzling out to nothing; they would never know any more than they knew now, and Ruth Traxler's considerable money would go to the man once known as Jerry Smith—whoever he really was or had been or was now. There wasn't anything anybody could do about it, and he'd better tell Charlene Garland so definitely and forget the whole thing. There was enough other business on hand. Unprecedentedly, when he'd got Davy to sleep Jesse went downstairs and made himself another drink.

* * *

About one o'clock the next morning two Beverly Hills patrolmen, Pollard and Isaacs, were cruising in a squad up Beverly Drive, when they got a call to unknown trouble. When they found the address, it was a big sprawling mansion beyond wide lawns, and it looked all dark; but there was a light showing at the end of a long drive and Isaacs pulled the squad in there and they walked up to the back door. There was a man lying on the floor of a big kitchen, and an elderly woman sitting in a chair at the kitchen table staring into space. She looked up at the tall uniformed men and she said, "It's the end of it now, and I better tell. I got to tell somebody about it."

They listened to her for five minutes and Pollard said, "Hell, this is a rigmarole for the front-office boys, and the night watch went off an hour ago. I guess they'll be roping Hollywood in too. And the damned detectives, they'll cuss us, but I suppose it can't wait till morning. You'd better get on the radio, Jim. I don't suppose the detectives'll want a lab treatment here, but you never know. And tell them they'll want a morgue wagon later on."

*   *   *

It was 10 A.M. when Clock and Petrovsky came to the Traxler house. The flat-faced housekeeper opened the door and as she recognized Clock her expression hardened to anger and fright and she stepped back. Clock had the badge out. He said, "We'd like to see Mr. Smith, or Mr. Traxler, or whatever he's calling himself."

From the door to the living room at the left, Ruth Traxler said in a chilly voice, "May I ask who you are, sir, and what you're doing in my house?"

Clock showed her the badge. "Sergeant Clock, LAPD, Mrs. Traxler." He looked back at the housekeeper. "His car's in the drive, so I know he's here. Go and get him." She started up the stairs without a word.

And Ruth Traxler, standing there tall and rigid, her English accent very pronounced, said icily, "My son's name is Mr. Traxler, Sergeant, and I cannot imagine why the police should be asking for him."

Clock said, "I'm very sorry to have to break it to you like this, Mrs. Traxler, but that's not his name. And he isn't Jerry Smith either. His name is Vince Oliver, he's twenty-nine years old, he's got a perfectly good mother and stepfather back in Ohio and an uncle right here. Up to three months ago, he was a professional blackjack dealer at a club in Las Vegas. And we want him for two homicides."

She just went on staring at him, her expression frozen. The housekeeper appeared at the top of the stairs and started slowly down, and Petrovsky said in an undertone, "Andrew—" Suddenly and without warning Ruth Traxler crumpled and fell, and the housekeeper came running to bend over her.

"I told you how it'd be, you come taking him away!" she said furiously. "What's the difference who he is, he made her happy—"

And they heard the snarl of the engine revved up outside, and Clock whirled for the front door with Petrovsky behind him. The Chrysler backed violently out of the drive and took off down the curving street, and Clock plunged back into the house and snapped at Petrovsky, "Find a phone and call in!"

"I told you how it'd be—and why wouldn't I tell him you're here, with your lies and tricks? And you'd better get a doctor and an ambulance before you do anything else—"

* * *

"We haven't taken a formal statement from her yet," said Clock. "I thought you'd like to sit in and hear the whole story." He was looking tired; he had already had a full day, and it wasn't over yet. Jesse and Gilchrist followed him silently through the communal detective office to the Captain's private office at the rear of the station. Kelsey wasn't there. She was sitting in an armchair by the window, and a uniformed man sat at the desk. Clock said, "We'd like to hear the whole story now. As I told you, we'll get it typed up for you to sign, and then we can take you back to the house to rest. It's been a long night, I know."

She said in a dragging voice, "I guess there'll be no rest for me, with all this happening. And Albert. And Albert. Yes, I'll tell you—just how it all happened. I know it was a wrong thing to do, from the beginning, and you always get punished for wrong things in the end." She was a big shapeless woman in a wrinkled cotton dress, cotton stockings, incongruous bedroom slippers on her feet. "I better go right back to the beginning and tell you how it all happened."

Clock said, "Just take your time, Mrs. Dutton."

"That's the first thing I got to tell you. I'm Mrs. Dillon, Thelma Dillon. I got to go back, all the way to when we worked for the Traxlers. We were there ten years, Albert and me, and it was a good place, they were good people to work for. The little boy came, and everybody in the house was that fond of him, the Traxlers ought to have known that. But when the trouble came, when he was kidnapped, it was like Mrs. Traxler went crazy. We were all sorry for them, we were all upset about the boy, and she hadn't any right to send us away like that, for no reason. Mr. Traxler knew that—he said to the woman at the agency, he'd see we got references—but it didn't do any good, because of the kidnapping. It was all on account of that, because we'd been there when it happened, people wouldn't hire us. It was a long time before we got work, and then it wasn't together, it was just odd jobs—and Albert couldn't let go of his grudge on Mrs. Traxler. It wasn't our fault about the kidnapping. Everything just falling to pieces for us, all of a sudden—and they never got the little boy back. And Albert said we'd never get decent jobs so long as people remembered, and we told that woman at the agency we were going back East, and we started calling ourselves Dutton, we went to another agency and told them we'd just come to California and we didn't have references because the lady we'd been with had died sudden. And they got us a job as a couple with some people in Pacific Palisades, so that was all right. We've been all right, we'd managed to save a little. And for the last five years we've been with the Osbornes in Beverly Hills, it's been a good job, an easy job. Mr. Osborne's got a lot of money, they aren't at the house in Beverly Hills but in the summer, they travel around a lot, a lot of the time they're at a place they own in Italy by a lake. When they come, they bring their own servants with them and there'll be a lot of parties and people coming. But when they're gone we're just there as caretakers like, there's a regular cleaning service once a month.

"Well, how—how it all started, I've got a brother here, Jim

Wheeler, and last November he broke his hip, and we'd go to visit him at the hospital. And he was in a room with another man broke his hip, a Robert Dunne, and Vince—Vince Oliver, he's Mr. Dunne's nephew. His mother had wrote and asked him to come over to see his uncle, make sure he's all right and gets moved back to his apartment. He'd come over from Las Vegas. And I haven't told you about that book, and maybe that was the real start of it." She was talking monotonously, slowly, and the uniformed man was taking it all down in rapid shorthand.

"I like a good read, I like detectives and murders and such. And I'd just got that book out of the library, all about unsolved mysteries, and it said in the front there was something about the Traxler case in it, and that was why I brought it from the library. And I was reading some about that to Albert, and it brought it all back to us. And he was still holding a grudge on that woman, even if we'd got on all right. Well, at the hospital we'd got sort of friendly with Vince, he's an easygoing friendly sort, anyways he acts it—you know, in the waiting room before visitors' hours and in the hospital room too. And Albert, he was telling him about the book and how we'd been in that house when the kidnapping happened. It was all Albert's idea, I got to say, but after a bit Vince was just as bad. Albert said it was funny, Vince kind of reminded him of somebody, and he said you know, it's that kid, the little Traxler kid, Vince was blond just like him, maybe the kid would've looked something like Vince when he grew up. He got the idea. He said to Vince, wouldn't it be a joke if you could make that woman think you was him, that you'd lost your memory and just now remembered who you was? It said in the book she'd never believed the kid was dead, I bet you she'd believe you and hand over a lot of money when she thought you was him. And first Vince just laughed and said there wouldn't be no chance, a lot of people knew who he was. Albert said we could tell him a lot—you know, things about the house and the boy when he was little, so she'd believe him. And after a while they both got thinking so hard about the money, they couldn't stop talking about how to do it. And one day—Vince had been coming to the house some

—he said he'd thought of a way that could work, so there'd be no way for anybody to find out who he really was. He said he'd been in the Army awhile back with this fellow named Jerry Smith, and this Smith, he told how he'd been raised in an orphanage right around here somewhere and nobody ever knew who he rightly was, what his real name was or nothing. And this Smith fellow was dead, he'd been killed in an accident when they was in the Army together, and he hadn't no what they call next of kin to notify, so nobody knew he was dead. And Vince said he could be him, and make it look like the kidnappers had left him somewhere and he lost his memory. He didn't know anybody here who knew who he really was, except his uncle, and he said he'd play up when he knew there was a lot of money in it."

"So simple when you know," murmured Gilchrist to Jesse.

"And it was his idea to say it was that book made him start to remember things about when he was a little kid. We told him all the things we could remember, about the house and about Tommy—and one thing I put in to make it sound even better—it said in the book, when that writer was talking to Mrs. Traxler, he sort of described the living room and said there was a picture of a French lady, I mean by some French artist, over the mantel and I knew that must've been changed because there used to be a picture with a wagon and horses in it—"

"Ye ironic gods!" said Gilchrist. "I'd forgotten that—just putting in local color."

"We were all thinking about the money then, see," she said painfully. "It wasn't just a joke, it was all that money she might give Vince. Everything she'd have given to Tommy. And he did it—he wrote her a letter, and she asked him to come to the house, and she believed him, she thought he was Tommy. Of course, Vince is a pretty good actor, and I guess now he'd been mixed up in some crooked things before. It didn't seem exactly crooked at first, but I knew it was all wrong—just for the money. And Vince said he'd give us a cut out of what she gave him. He got all set with her, everything worked out just fine, just like him and Albert thought—and then that girl showed up. See, when all this happened, he'd given his uncle our phone number, in case he wanted to reach Vince—"

"Robert Dunne," said Clock under his breath, "down on Eleventh Street."

And Jesse said, "My God, that's where he was going when Allen lost him that night."

"And Mr. Dunne didn't know what to do when that Fisher girl showed up looking for Vince. Vince, he'd given her his uncle's address, of course he didn't know when he came over here he'd be staying, and fixing himself up to be Tommy Traxler the rest of his life—and Dunne, he gave her our number. We had an arrangement with Vince, if we wanted to talk to him Albert would call the house on Wednesday afternoon, that was when Mrs. Traxler went to her bridge club. And Albert told him about the girl, and he cussed and said he'd get rid of her some way. She'd left a number for him to call—she was good and mad at him, said he owed her some money—Sally Fisher her name was—but I guess he paid her off and that satisfied her, so that was all right. The old lady's niece tried to make some trouble, she got a lawyer, but Vince said there wasn't anything they could do—it was all working out fine. But the money—it was all the money made the trouble—Albert said all the money Mrs. Traxler had, and believing he was Tommy and all, she'd be handing over a lot of money to him, like a big allowance—we knew she'd bought him that fancy car—and he was only sending us a measly twenty-five a week and Albert was mad. He kept calling Vince and saying he better pay us a lot more, he couldn't never have made her believe him if it hadn't been for us and what we could tell him—and Vince said she wasn't giving him much cash, only like credit cards and such, but Albert didn't believe him. And he said, Albert did I mean, there'd have to be a showdown, we wasn't going to stand it. He told Vince if he didn't pay up better we'd go and tell Mrs. Traxler the truth and that'd be the end of all the money—and Vince said all right, he'd come and see us and explain just how things was. And he came—last night—and he was mad at both of us, he said that goddamned lawyer had put a tail on him, it had to be the lawyer, only he didn't think at night, but it was too risky for us ever to meet, and he said all over again how she didn't give him much cash, but he gave Albert a hundred dollars and Albert called him a damn cheapskate and Vince called him a name and said it didn't matter if we went to Mrs. Traxler, she'd never believe us and he had her just where he wanted her, and he got up to go and Albert tried to hit him, and Vince just knocked him down against the table and went out. I went and got a wet towel, I thought Albert was just knocked out a minute or two—but he started breathing awful funny—and after a while he—well, he just died. I felt him die right under my hand. And I knew—I knew it was all finished—and I had to tell. I had to tell all about it, so it couldn't go on—doing such a wrong thing. So I called the police. And I guess that's all." She just sat there silent then, sagging in the chair.

* * *

Outside the office, Clock said, "Unless he talks, we'll never know just how the Fisher girl got murdered. He probably arranged to meet her somewhere to pay her off and get rid of her, and I'd have a guess that when she saw the car he was driving, she guessed he'd stumbled onto a gold mine somehow and wanted a piece of the action. Possibly they had a fight in the car —anyway, he ended up strangling her. He probably cleaned out her motel room, took her purse—the only thing he missed was that card in her pocket, and of course we were misled on that."

"Catalytic agents!" said Jesse. "My God, A meets B and there's an explosion! Do we blame fate? If the hospital hadn't put those two in the same room—"

"And what a beautifully simple plot," said Gilchrist.

"I don't suppose he had any intention of killing Dillon," said Jesse. "He was just unlucky enough to knock him down against a heavy table."

"That's about it," said Clock. "It was probably a skull fracture —the autopsy will say."

"What's going to happen to Mrs. Dillon?" asked Gilchrist.

Clock shrugged. "It'll be up to Mrs. Traxler, if she wants to prosecute for fraud. I don't think she will. She's in the hospital with a mild heart attack, I understand."

"Well, I hope you pick him up," said Jesse.

"We will," said Clock grimly, "we will."

* * *

Forty-eight hours later, on a state highway in New Mexico, a state trooper by the name of Castillo was cruising on tour when a big red Chrysler came around the squad in a legal pass. It was wearing a California plate, and Castillo glanced at it from force of habit, and got a second look before the Chrysler got too far ahead. He reached for the list of posted A.P.B. plate numbers on the dashboard. He thought that had rung a bell; there was a want on the Chrysler from California. He switched on the siren and started after it, and the Chrysler took off like a scalded cat.

Four miles down the straight-as-an-arrow road the Chrysler came up on a plodding big truck hauling a load of gravel. Castillo braked and slowed. Up ahead in the two-lane road a pickup truck and a car were in the other lane. The driver of the Chrysler took the chance that he could get past in time, and poured on the gas, pulling alongside the truck. He had misjudged the speed of the pickup. As he started to pull around the truck, time and space ran out and the Chrysler hit the pickup head on with a noise like a bomb. Before the sound had died the oncoming car rammed into both of them with brakes squealing, and all three slid across the road into the drainage ditch on one side.

Castillo said, "Jesus Christ!" and braked the squad, reaching for the radio to call an ambulance. The driver of the gravel truck braked and came back to see if he could help.

The couple in the pickup were very messily dead; the man in the other car was just barely alive. When they pried the driver of the Chrysler out of the wreckage, oddly enough his face wasn't touched at all; he was a young good-looking blond fellow and his neck was broken.

* * *

Jesse was wrestling with some paper work the following Friday afternoon when Jean put through a call. "This is Forslund," said a young male voice.

"Sorry, who?"

"Oh, I forgot you won't know my name. The intern you were talking to at St. Joseph's hospital the other day."

"Oh, yes."

"I called to tell you that that Carnahan's dead. He died just a couple of hours ago. And he left you a note or a letter or something. He didn't know your name, he just told the nurse it was for that lawyer—but as it happened I still had your card. I just clipped it onto the note and left it at the nurses' station for you."

"So, thanks," said Jesse. He was curious enough to go all the way out there on his way home, to get it.

It was a plain sealed envelope with nothing written on it. He stood there in the hospital corridor and ripped it open, took out a plain sheet of cheap paper folded once. There were just four words in the center of the sheet in big shaky printing

The feds were right

* * *

It was at the end of June that he ushered a client out one afternoon to find Charlene Garland in the waiting room. "I won't take five minutes, Mr. Falkenstein."

"That's all right," and he took her into his office. She was looking, as usual, smart and attractive.

"I just thought you'd be interested to know that Aunt Ruth is dead. She died last week. She got better after that attack she had—when he was found out—but she wasn't ever really strong again, and she died last Thursday. The funeral was on Monday."

"I'm sorry to hear that," said Jesse conventionally.

"You needn't be, you know—I think she was ready to go. She'd made a new will—after that. She's left everything to me, the house and everything else."

"Well, that's good news at least."

She hadn't sat down. "Yes, isn't it? The very first thing I'm going to do is clear out that nursery and see that everything in it is burned."

"That's a good idea, it should have been done long ago."

"Yes," she said. "And I found out about that body, you know —Aunt Ruth told me about it just before she died. Uncle Tom claimed it and bought a plot out in Rose Hills Cemetery. I'm going to see that a headstone's put up."

"Do you think that's necessary?" he asked gently.

"I think Uncle Tom and Aunt Ruth would like it," she said definitely. "I just wanted to thank you again for everything you've done, Mr. Falkenstein."

"I didn't really do much, you know."

"And I thought I'd go and see that nursemaid—Miss Drake. I always liked her, and I know she'd want to know—about Tommy."

"She'd appreciate that. I think I've still got her address somewhere."

And five minutes later, as he watched her out, he felt that at last the lost restless little ghost of Tommy Traxler was laid, and at rest.

He went out to the anteroom and got his hat. He said to his Gordons, "I'm taking off early, girls. You might as well too. Tomorrow's another day."

LESLEY EGAN is a pseudonym for a popular, very prolific author of mysteries. Her most recent novels are RANDOM DEATH, THE MISER and A CHOICE OF CRIMES.

M

```
Fic       Egan, Lesley
E             Little boy lost ⌐1st ed⌐ Garden City,
          New York, Doubleday, 1983.
              179 p.

A26410    DD Crime Club    7/83     $5.00    (11.95)
          NO OTHER CARDS.
```